YAHZIE-APACHE WARRIOR

BOOK EIGHT OF THE TYE WATKINS SERIES

Gary McMillan

Cover concept and design by Michael McMillan

Copyrighted April, 2012

ISBN Number 0-9844730-7-6

Published by Authors Discovery Inc.
2645 Kermit highway
Odessa, Texas 79763
432-553-2308

Printed in the United States of America

Tye Watkins is Chief of Scouts at Fort Clark, Texas. His father, Ben, had been a well know mountain man back in the days of the beaver craze in the Rockies. When the demand for beaver furs died in the mid 1830's, Ben left the Rockies to go to the new Republic of Texas where land was plentiful. In San Antonio he fell in love and got himself hitched to a lady named Lori. They homesteaded in southwest Texas near the Rio Grande which is the boundary between Texas and Mexico. In 1839, they had a son and named him Tyrone-Tye for short.

Ben begin to teach Tye how to shoot, hunt, trap, track and fight when the boy was old enough to walk. In the years since his father was killed, Tye had honed these lessons until he was considered the best scout in Texas, feared by the bandits and respected as a great warrior by the Apache.

Shakespeare McDovitt, nicknamed Buff, is a seventy one year old ex-mountain man who was Tye's father's best friend back in those days in the Rockies. The last few years he had been scouting for the army in Colorado, and kept hearing reports from soldiers coming from Texas to Colorado about this scout in Texas named Watkins whose father had been a mountain man. Since his only regret in life had been he had not gone to Texas to see his friend Ben before he had been killed, he decided to meet his son. He now lives on the fort with Tye and Tye's wife, Rebecca.

The event everyone on the fort has waited for was here, the arrival of Tye's and Rebecca's first baby. The happy event was short lived though as trouble once again reared it's ugly head. Two men, half dead stumbled into the fort and reported they had been wounded and their friends killed by the Apache. This was not an uncommon event given the times, but being winter and no reported trouble for awhile raised Tye's suspicions as to the validity of the men's story. Also, the fact that the men said there was only one Apache that killed four of their friends and wounded both of them only raised his suspicions more. Tye was dispatched to see if the men's story was true and if so, find the Apache responsible.

He would find out the men's story was half true. He would also learn there was a reason for the Apache's hostility. The next few days would be the most dangerous of Tye's life: tracking the Apache, Yazhie. Added to the danger was a man named Zeb Cates who was intent on killing the scout for his part in the deaths of his nephews, Yancey and Billy Cates. Yancey and Billy had been ex-Confederate soldiers who hated anything that wore blue uniforms. They were also vicious killers who preyed on the homesteaders and Tye had tracked them down, and along with a troop of soldiers, killed all the gang members including Billy, and captured Yancey who was eventually hung.

Dedication

Yahzie is dedicated to my wife of 33 years, Debbie whose love and understanding allows me the private time to do what I love to do, write stories about the Old West.

Books in the Tye Watkins Series

Border Trouble
The Crossing
Yancey
The Desperate Trail
Drums Along the Border
Back To the Rockies
Second Chance
Yazhie-Apache Warrior

Chapter One

The first day of December dawned cloudy, cold, and with just a trace of falling snow. It promised to be a cold, dreary, and miserable day for the troops at Fort Clark. However, in the forts hospital, things could not be merrier. It had been a long night for Rebecca, Tye, Buff, the O'Malley's, as well as Major Thurston and a great number of soldiers. Rebecca had given birth to a five-and-a-half pound little boy, and to everyone's surprise, a baby girl that weighed a little under five pounds. The mother and both babies were doing fine. The only casualties were Tye and Buff: both nervous wrecks.

Loud cheers had arisen from the troopers when Mrs. O'Malley brought the news that it was a boy. With all the back slapping and shouting, a man would have thought there was free beer to be had. She quieted the men down and told them about the little girl. There was a moment of dead silence and then as one, the troops whooped it up again at the news. A chorus of hip-hip-hoorays followed. The troops loved Rebecca and Tye and each had looked forward to this moment. One thing was for sure; Tye and Rebecca would never be short of someone to watch the babies.

Mrs. O'Malley was happier than she had been in a long time. Even her husband, crusty old Sergeant Major O'Malley, was even a little misty eyed over the event.

Tye was behind the curtain, seeing his wife and for the first time, his son and daughter. Buff was standing off by himself, feeling a little left out, when Tye stuck his head out from behind the curtain.

"Hey Buff...come here you old coot and see your grandkids." Buff hurried over and Tye held the baby boy out for him to hold. Buff hesitated, trying to get his arms in the right position so the baby would fit. His efforts gave Mrs. O'Malley, Tye, and Rebecca a good laugh.

Mrs. O'Malley hurried over to Buff and from behind the old mountain man, using her hands, placed his arms in the right position. Tye placed the baby in his arms and everyone thought Buff was going to faint.

"Wh...what if'n I drop him?"

"You aren't going to drop him you old codger," Mrs. O'Malley said laughing. She took Buff by the elbows and moved his arms back and forth in a rocking motion. The baby took Buff's finger in his tiny hand and a smile as big as the Rockies spread across the weathered face of the old trapper. A couple of tears trailed down his cheeks as well. At any other time he would have been embarrassed, but not this particular one. He was holding a baby for the first time in his life and watching a seventy-one year old man holding a baby for the first time was a moment everyone embraced.

Tye and Rebecca had discussed a thousand names the last few months trying to come up with the proper one. They always came back to the one they both knew was the right one-Anthony Benjamin Watkins…Ben for short, after Tye's father, and Anthony for Rebecca's father. If the baby was a girl, the name would be Nicole Watkins, after Rebecca's mother. After a few minutes of Buff spoiling Ben, Tye took him from Buff's arms, and walked around the curtains so everyone could get a look. Mrs. O'Malley held Nicole for all to see.

Tough old Sergeant O'Malley was the first in line…after the major of course, to make a fuss over little Ben and Nicole. The men came by one at a time and looked at the babies and tickled them with their fingers. Tye watched the expressions on their faces and chuckled. Most of them were veterans of many Apache skirmishes and tough as they come. Little Ben and Nicole made them act like silly children with all the facial expressions and the noises they made trying to be the first to get a smile from the babies.

After the last soldier had his turn, Tye took little Ben and Nicole back to his mother. He laid their babies, one in each arm, and then with his fingers, brushed Rebecca's damp hair from her forehead and kissed her there. He kissed her on the end of the nose and then on the lips whispering all the while how much he loved her. Mrs. O'Malley looked at Buff and motioned with her head indicating they should leave the two alone for a few minutes. Tye, after the two left, lay down on the bed beside his wife and babies.

"I love you Honey," he whispered in her ear, "and I'm so proud."

"You will never know the depth of my love for you, Tye. It is something that is so deep I don't have the words to express."

They hugged for a few minutes and Tye said. "You and the baby…I mean babies need to get some rest. I'll be back in a couple hours or so." He kissed her on the cheek. "Go to sleep," he said and kissed Ben on the head, then Nicole.

"Tye," Rebecca said, grabbing his hand, "You're not upset because it was twins are you?"

Tye smiled as he placed his hand on her forehead. "Honey, I've never been happier in my whole life. I swear." He kissed her on the lips. "Now get some rest."

After leaving the hospital, the O'Malley's went home and Buff and Tye walked on to their house.

"It's been quite a day already hasn't it," Buff said.

Tye chuckled. "It has at that, Buff. It's been the best day of my life."

"Things are good alright," Buff chuckled. "Rebecca's fine, you have a baby boy and girl, I'm a grandpa, and everything is quite on the fort. The Apache and the bandits must have known your babies were coming because they haven't been any trouble reported."

"I've been here all my life Buff, and I've learned one thing: trouble is always just around the corner. Just about the time you think things are good…they change. You can't ever let yourself get comfortable." He stopped walking and stared off in the distance. "I think that is why I love it so much. Living is such a challenge every day."

"I can relate to that. That's the way it was in the Rockies when your pa and me were trapping beaver.

Danger and uncertainty will make one appreciate living that much more."

Tye looked at Buff and shook his head. Buff noticed the look and asked. "What's wrong?"

Tye laughed and slapped the old mountain man on the shoulder. "Nothing is the matter old friend. What you just said made me think of something. When I'm on scout…all alone and knowing danger is close, that's when I feel the most alive. Is that strange or what?"

"You know something…that's exactly what I heard old Jim Bridger say one time when we were in deep trouble with a bunch of Blackfeet. We knew they were close, but didn't know how many or what they were going to do. That's when Jim smiled and made that statement. At the time I thought is was one of his dumbest ever," Buff said chuckling then added, "He was right, though."

Just as the two reached the porch of their home, they heard someone hollering. Looking back they saw Private Carter coming toward them as fast as his legs would carry him.

"So much for it being quiet," Tye muttered.

Stopping a few feet from the men on the porch, Carter, trying to catch his breath said, "Big trouble, Tye. The major wants you at headquarters right away."

Tye turned to Buff. "I'll be back soon." Buff nodded.

Trotting toward post headquarters, Tye asked. "What's going on, Adam?"

"All I know is that two men came into Brackett half dead. They were taken to Thurston and a few minutes later he came out of his office and told me to get your ass here pronto."

Chapter Two

A hundred miles east of Fort Clark, Zeb Cates sat beside his fire, drinking coffee, mulling over why he was camped on this creek in the middle of nowhere. He was forty-five years old and a veteran of the big War. He had lost everything in the War; his family, his slaves, and his wealth. He lost his family's plantation to the damn carpetbaggers that came after the War, claiming everything under the New Reconstruction Government. He had friends and relatives killed during the war and some after the war. Two of them that were killed after the war were the reason he was where he was now. His two nephews, Yancey and Billy Cates, had been killed by a man named Tye Watkins who was a scout at Fort Clark, Texas.

He knew all about Yancey and Billy. He knew they rode with Quantrill and had been involved in some terrible crimes against civilians, both during and after the War. He had strong feelings against the Yankees but not to the extent that he wanted to still kill all of them like his nephews had. The two had killed indiscriminately, men, women, and children and he didn't approve, but blood was thick and he intended to make life miserable for this scout before killing him.

Zeb, unlike Yancey and Billy, was an intimidating man to look at. He stood three inches over six feet and weighed over two hundred pounds. He was broad at the shoulders, thick through the chest, and narrow at the hips. His arms were like steel from swinging a hammer. Since the War, he had been trying his hand at blacksmithing and had become quite good at it.

News traveled slowly and it was several months after Yancey and Billy were killed before he heard about their deaths. He was never one to act without thinking things out and he fretted for several days trying to decide what he would do. When he did decide, he left his blacksmith business and headed to Texas to revenge the killings

In the War, Zeb showed he was a natural leader and had quickly risen to the rank of captain in the Confederate Army. He had participated in several skirmishes with the Yankees and was considered a great tactician and was known to be completely fearless in battle. He wasn't sure how he was going to kill this scout, but he was confident he would figure out a way. Standing up, he emptied his cup, covered the fire with dirt, saddled his horse and headed west.

~~

Thurston was waiting on the porch at Post Headquarters when Carter arrived with Tye.

"What's the problem, Major?"

"I hate the timing of this Tye with the new babies, but I just spoke with two men that were badly wounded. Their group was attacked by an Apache.

"An Apache?"

Thurston nodded. "That's what they said…one Apache."

"How many men were with them?"

"Four. They were killed over a two day period. Seems, this Apache stalked them and killed them one at a time."

"Where did all take place?"

"They're at the hospital. Let's go see them and you can ask what you want."

Less than five minutes later they were with the two men whose wounds were being treated by the post surgeon.

"I'll be thru in a minute, Major, and then they're all yours," the Post Surgeon, Captain McCann said." Thurston nodded and he and Tye stepped back to wait. Tye was sizing the men up and didn't like what he saw. They were not dressed as trappers or hunters and seeing the smoothness of their hands, knew they did not do manual labor such as farming, ranching, or mining. Their guns on their hips looked well taken care of though.

"I'll be back in a minute, Major." He walked outside to look at the men's horses. Both horses were top of the line stock. Looking through their saddlebags he found the usual: extra shirt and pants, tobacco and makings for cigarettes, extra shells, matches, coffee cup, plate, fork and spoon, and cash...a hell of lot of cash. After placing everything back, he went back inside to where the major waited. He had more questions now than he had a few minutes ago. The surgeon had left and Thurston stood beside the chairs the men were sitting on. He introduced Tye to the men.

"This is my Chief of Scouts, Tye Watkins. Tye, this here is Joe Daly and Billy Hunter." The men shook hands.

"Heard of you," the one named Billy said as he shook Tye's hand. The one named Joe did not say anything, but his eyes kept going from Tye to the major and back to Tye.

He had what Tye said was nervous eyes, a common trait of a lot of outlaws he had brought in.

"Where did this attack happen?"

Billy spoke. "It started about forty or so miles on the other side of Eagle's nest. The last time we were attacked was where the Pecos and Rio Grande Rivers meet. We were trying to get to the fort to report the trouble."

"Major Thurston said you told him there was just one Apache." Billy hung his headed and mumbled.

"That's the sad truth…only one damn Apache, but he is the devil himself. I don't know how many times we all shot at him and never hit him. He stayed after us and killed us one at a time…and taking his damn pleasure in doing it I would guess."

"You're telling me there were six of you, all armed, and one Apache who wounded the two of you and killed four of your friends," Tye stated, his tone of voice betraying his doubting the story.

"That's what we are saying," Billy said. Tye looked at the nervous eyed Joe who nodded his head indicating his agreement.

"Where are the bodies of your friends?"

"The last one was killed as we rode up the trail leading out of the canyon where the Rio Pecos and the Rio

Grande meet. That's where we were hit also. The Apache is an expert shot. He hit Jarrod, that's our friend that was killed, and hit both of us from the top of the opposite rim. The shots must have been close to two hundred yards.

"Did he have a Sharps?"

"As many shots as he was firing it must have been a Henry repeater."

Tye nodded. "You men get some rest. I'll check into the matter." Tye looked at Thurston. He decided not to ask about the money. Asking would raise their suspicions as to why he went through their belongings. "Let's go to your office, major."

When they left the hospital Tye muttered. "That was the biggest bunch of horseshit I have ever heard."

Thurston stopped. "What do you mean?"

"We don't know these men, Major. They're not trappers or hunters and sure as hell not cowhands, farmers or anyone else that works."

"How do you know this?"

"It ain't hard. First of all, look at their clothes and second, their hands. They haven't done an honest days work in a long time and they ain't wearing cheap clothes. They have horses that are top stock and they have close to a thousand dollars in their saddlebags."

"You went through their saddlebags?" Thurston expressed with a surprised look on his face.

"There's a lot more to this story than just an Apache trailing and killing them and that story about the two hundred yard shot is more dung. A Henry is not accurate at that range. An old Sharp would be, but not a Henry. Their story is full of holes and I'm guessing you'll want me to find the answers to plug them?"

Thurston nodded. "I see what you mean about the holes, but as Post Commander it is my responsibility to check out all the stories that come in. One thing we know for sure…they were both shot up."

"I'll be leaving in a couple hours. Would it be possible for me to take three or four men with me?"

"Tell me who you want and I will get them for you as well as supplies for a week."

Tye mentioned some names and then headed back to the hospital to see Rebecca. He knew she wasn't going to be happy with the news of his leaving so soon after Ben and Nicole being born.

Chapter Three

Tye sat on Sandy looking down at the body of the man he figured to be Jarrod, the friend of Billy and Joe. Half of his head was blown away and the bullet apparently hit him in the forehead and exited out the back. *That doesn't go along with their story of being shot at from the rim behind them,* Tye mused. He looked at the top of the rim across the canyon and knew their story was a lie.

"It's *got to be two hundred and fifty yards at least,* he noted. *Too kill a man from that distance and wound two that were on running horses would take the best marksman I ever saw and most Apaches I have encountered are not expert marksman. On top of that, no way a Henry was effective at that distance."*

Stepping down from Sandy, Tye went through the dead mans pockets. They were empty, not even the makings for a smoke. *"An Apache might have taken the tobacco,* he mused, *but not the paper."* He remembered the men did not have an extra horse with them and looking around, saw none. *"Taking the horse is the only thing that even hints that this was done by an Apache."* The fact the other men had money and he found none in the pockets of the corpse also indicated it was someone other than an Apache. *"If there's one thing in the world an Apache has no use for is white man's money."* He turned to Corporal Absher.

"Get the men to scratch out a hole and put the body in and then pile some rocks on it to keep the varmints away. Corporal Absher and three men, Private Jacobson, Private Abernathy, and Private Carter were the men with Tye.

Tye mounted Sandy and splashed across the shallow Pecos River. He rode up the canyon to the rim to get a view of what the warrior would have had as he shot at the white men.

Looking across the canyon to where the body had been laying, Tye pondered the situation. *"No way in hell could that Apache have hit three men…one maybe with a lucky shot but not three?"* Looking around on the ground as he walked back and forth along the rim, he found five shell casings….yellow boys, forty-four caliber rim fire which is what the Henry uses. They were called yellow boys because of the brass casings. He re-mounted Sandy and rode back to where the men were burying the man he had been told was named Jarrod. Absher had found a flat rock and scratched some words.

Jarrod

Kilt by Apaches

December 1 1870

Tye nodded his approval and dismounted. Looking around he found tracks of two horses, one shod and one unshod. Following them to where they entered the shallow waters of the Rio Grande he looked across the river and saw where they came out of the water. He waded across and studied the tracks in the sand. Standing up he followed them with his eyes till they disappeared around a bend in the river. He followed the tracks and saw where they re-entered the water and exited once again on the Texas side. He waded back to the men.

"There are only a few minutes of good light left," he told the men. "Let's make camp back up on the rim in that old burned out homestead. We can build a fire inside the walls and stay a little warmer." Leading Sandy up the trail to the rim he remembered the Freeman's, the family that lived in the homestead. They were killed by that damn blood-thirsty Yancey Cates and his gang about a year or so ago.

Chapter Four

The chill of another fall night set in as the sun disappeared and darkness settled in over the Texas landscape. Yahzie shivered slightly before the small fire began to hold off the chill from his body. As he sat beside the fire, a blanket wrapped around his shoulders, he reflected on the recent events that led him here. He was alone; far from the coziness of his wickiup and his only belongings were his rifle, pistol, knife, and horse.

He was an Apache, a Mescalero warrior and had proven himself fearless in battle with the Comanche, Mexicans, and the white man. He had taken many scalps and counted coup many times from his people's enemies and yet, as tough as he was, a tear rolled down his cheek as he dwelled on the events of the past week

Six white men had ridden into his camp while he was away hunting. They killed his father and mother, raped and killed his wife, and bashed his young son's head in with a rifle butt. They had even shot his ponies that were grazing nearby. He followed the men and had killed them one at a time until only two were left alive and he knew both of them were wounded, and possibly dead. He had not followed the two wounded men because of Fort Clark being near. He did not want to risk stumbling onto soldiers from there.

All he had in life had been taken from him by these men in just a few minutes. He had nothing now, just the memories of his parents, and the son that would never grow to become an Apache warrior. He thought of his woman, her love for him, and his for her; her warm body that he would never embrace again; the harmony and happiness that had now been replaced by hate. This hate burned in his belly like a fire that would never be put out. He stared at the flickering flames and swore he would kill every white man he came across, man, woman and child. Let them feel how he now felt-empty and lost, with nothing to live for.

His thoughts went to his father, and the stories he would tell around the camp fires. Stories about when the Apache rode this land as they wished, without worry someone would come into their camp and kill their loved ones while the young men were away. Then, the Mexicans and the white men began taking their land and killing the Apache on sight. At first, the Apache tried to be friends with the white man but their greed and their lies quickly harden the Apache hearts. Now, it had been war for several winters and the Apache, who were few in number, were losing their land-and their freedom.

His friends had wanted to go with him on his chase of the men who killed his family, but he had insisted he would go alone. He wanted to kill each man himself. Reflecting back, he wished he had let some of them come with him. With them, he could now inflict much more damage to the white eyes than he could alone.

Standing up, he walked over to his pony and while scratching the neck of his mount, looked up at the stars and the new moon. Staring at the night sky, a thought struck him.

"The Apache is like the moon, all alone, and surrounded by the stars who are like the white men, too many to count." He walked back to the small fire and lay down, an empty feeling inside him.

"My family is gone…and soon the Apache way of life will be no more. Before that day comes, I will make Yahzie

a name the white man will remember forever." He smiled for the first time in days at the thought, and drifted off into a restive sleep.

~~

Tye lay under his army issue wool blanket starring at the moon and stars. Sleep was hard to come by this night as a lot of worrisome things were going through his mind.

"*Things just don't add up,*" he thought. "*Why would a lone Apache track, kill, and wound six armed white men? How could a single warrior do this? Were the two wounded men lying about the last man, Jarrod's, death? They said he was killed while they rode out of the canyon, but the bullet that killed him appeared to come from the front, not the rear. Where did the money in the men's saddlebags come from? If the men were fleeing this crazy Apache, why would they stop and go through the man's pockets and remove money and valuables? The only thing that made any sense was the fact the man's horse was gone; an Apache would not pass up a chance at a horse. A lot of damn questions,*" he thought, "*And right now, I don't have a single stinking answer.*" He sat up.

"Trouble sleeping?" Corporal Absher whispered. Corporal Absher was a friend of Tye's besides being one hell of a soldier. Absher's grandpa had trapped beaver in the Rockies with Tye's pa many years ago.

"Yeah. I'm trying to figure out what went on between this Apache and six white men. Something tells me there's a lot more to this than just a warrior suddenly tracking down six men, killing four of them."

"Been doing some thinking about that myself," Absher said. "Things don't add up to what you said those men told you and the major. I didn't say anything back where we buried Jarrod, but I'm more than a fair shot with a rifle and where that man was killed and the other two wounded took one hell of marksman."

"I know it, especially since it was a Henry the Indian was using. That's a hell of a long shot for one of those rifles. Besides, it appeared to me he was shot from the front."

After a few seconds, Absher spoke. "By God, you're right now that I think about it. He wasn't shot from behind. What do you make of it?"

"It's pretty obvious to me those two are lying about some of the facts. I don't doubt their story about the Apache, but I think the killing shot on the man named Jarrod came from one of them. I think they emptied his pockets also. He was wounded pretty badly earlier and they may have shot him to put him out of his misery, or they killed him because he was slowing them down and they panicked. The third possibility is they just plain murdered him. They had a lot of cash in their saddlebags and I'll bet my life they didn't acquire it honestly."

Absher scratched the back of his neck. "It's hard for me to believe one Apache could do what they said."

"I've encountered some warriors that could do it. Remember this Absher; an Apache is not like a white man when it comes to dying; they are not afraid to die. That fact is what makes them what they are; the best fighting men in the world. A general once commented that if the Apache had as many warriors as the Comanche, all of Texas would still belong to them. So yeah, as hard as it is to believe, I wouldn't discount their story about the one Apache completely-not yet anyway." He lay back down. "Let's get some sleep."

~~

Zeb Cates had covered a lot of miles today. Lying under his blanket beside the small fire he was doing some thinking. *"I probably covered thirty or more miles today. I figure I may be only sixty or so miles from Fort Clark and that damn scout. I could be there day after tomorrow.* He looked up at the stars. *"The sky looks the same as back home, but looking at this land, it ain't fit for nothing. I can't believe people are coming out here to live. They should just leave the sinking Injun's alone and let them have the land. From what I have seen, I wouldn't give a wooden nickel for all of it."* He rolled over his side and pulled the wool blanket tight around his shoulders. *"Oh well. I ain't gonna be out here long."* He drifted off to sleep thinking of how he was going to kill Watkins. What ever way it was would be slow.

Chapter Five

An hour after sunrise, Yahzie lay on his stomach behind some cedars watching a white man and his son preparing to go to the field to work. They walked, leading a horse that pulled a wagon with what the white man called a plow on it. As he watched, the man and boy stopped and lifted the plow off the wagon and placed it behind the horse. They were no more than forty yards from where Yahzie lay.

Yahzie took aim with his Henry and squeezed the trigger. The bullet struck the man square in the chest, knocking him to the ground. The boy, standing with a look of disbelief over his father, would be an easy kill for the warrior. He again aimed the Henry and slowly squeezed the trigger. He stopped when he heard the boy's mother's footsteps as she ran toward them. Yahzie moved the barrel to the right and pulled the trigger. The woman stopped, dropped to the ground and stood back up, took a step, wavered, and then fell face first to the ground.

Yahzie stood up and the boy saw him immediately. He walked toward the boy who did not run away. As he walked toward the boy, the youngster bent down and picked up a rock and threw it at the warrior. Yahzie dodged the rock and then another as the boy picked up more of them and threw them. When they were only five feet apart the boy, who appeared to be about ten winters old, simply stood there, hate showing in his eyes, Yahzie pulled his knife half way out of its sheath and then dropped it back in.

Yahzie looked at the boy and thought. *"Boy is brave, like Apache boy. He no cry.* He turned and walked away. Looking back, he saw the boy sitting on the ground, his mother's head in his lap. As full of hate as Yahzie was, when it came down to it, he could not bring himself to kill a child. He mounted his pony and rode north, where another homestead he knew of was located.

~~

Mid-morning found Yahzie, lying on his stomach on top of a small hill, watching two white men and a Mexican squatted in a small stream. They were looking for the shiny metal that he knew other men had found in streams like this one. He knew the metal was worth something to the white man, but he had no use for it other than it made pretty necklaces that the women like to wear.

The men had their back to him and the little noise the fast moving stream made would drown out any sound he made. He checked his rifle and moved down the slope. As he figured, they were too busy and the stream to loud for them to hear him. He stood ten feet from them for a full minute before one stood up and turned around a saw him. Yahzie was the last thing he saw as a bullet smashed into his forehead. One of the other men reached for his pistol, but was too slow. A bullet from the warrior's rifle hit him in the chest and blood spewed out as the bullet exploded out of his back. He was dead when he hit the water. The third man, the Mexican, his eyes wide with fear, raised his hands much to the disgust of Yahzie. There is nothing an Apache hates more than a coward.

Motioning with the rifle, Yahzie indicated for the man to come out of the water, drop his gun from the holster, and sit. When the Mexican was seated, Yazhie kneeled and with his hand, dipped some water to drink. Speaking in Spanish, Yahzie spoke.

"I am Yahzie, Mescalero Apache. Remember that name well. Men like you have killed my family, and now, I will kill as many of you as I can." He then shot the man in the left leg, just above the knee. The Mexican writhed on the ground in agony. Yazhie stepped forward and grabbed him by the hair. Bending down and getting in the man's face, he repeated. "My name is Yazhie. Remember it." He loosened his grip on the man's hair and the injured man fell back on the ground. Yahzie spit on him and walked away.

~~

The Apache was making no effort to cover his tracks as Tye and his men followed them. From the tracks, Tye figured they were a half-day behind the warrior. Tye was stopping only long enough to give the horses a short blow every hour or so. It was mid-afternoon when Tye reined in Sandy.

A short distance ahead of them was a homestead, but that was not what had Tye's attention. He saw a small boy digging and what looked to be two bodies wrapped in blankets. The boy spotted him at the same time and picked up a rifle.

"Its okay son, we're friendly." Tye shouted. The boy held the rifle with the barrel pointing at the men. "My name is Tye Watkins. I am a scout at Fort Clark and these men with me are soldiers there."

The boy, noticing for the first time the men were dressed in the blue uniforms of the cavalry, lowered his gun. Tye and the men nudged their mounts toward the boy. Tye dismounted and walked to the boy. "What happened?" he asked seeing there were bodies in the blankets. Tye already figured who the dead people were. It was obvious the boy had been crying.

"Apache shot my ma and pa this morning," he said, his voice trembling. Tye kneeled down and pulled the youngster to his chest, hugging him for a full minute. The boy quit trembling and Tye pushed him back just a bit but kept both his hands on the boy's shoulders.

"Let's me and you go into the house," Tye said. He turned and looked at Absher and nodded toward the bodies. Absher understood and he and the men dismounted. Private Abernathy picked up the shovel and started digging while mumbling something about a damn Apache.

Private Carter picked up another shovel he found leaning against the corral fence and began helping Abernathy.

"What do you make of it?" he asked Absher.

"We have one pissed off Apache I'd say," the corporal stated. He's killed six people that we know of and wounded two more."

Carter stopped digging. "Why didn't he kill the boy too?"

"Dunno for sure, but Tye said that a lot of times an Apache will not kill a youngster if the kid shows some spunk and not whimper like a baby. I'm guessing the boy showed some of that."

Inside the house, Tye was smiling. Not smiling at what had happened to the lads parents, but at what the boy had told him about throwing rocks at the killer of his parents. He now knew why the Apache did not kill him also. Tye had noticed the corral, the outhouses, and the house; all were well built and kept up. The house was clean and everything in its place. It reminded him of his old homestead which he went by often and kept in good repair, including his parents graves.

"Looks like you pa kept everything in good shape," he hesitated a second. "What is your name anyway?"

"Robert…Robert Spencer," the boy replied.

"And your ma and pa's"?

"John and Elizabeth," he said as tears welled up in his eyes and rolled down his cheeks.

Tye looked up as Absher stuck his head in the door. "Do you kno…"

"John and Elizabeth Spencer," Tye said knowing what Absher was going to ask. Absher nodded and shut the door.

Tye picked up the boy and carried him over to a bed and laid him on it. "I'll be back in a minute," he said patting the boy on the head.

Stepping outside, he walked over to where the men were standing by the graves. Absher was carving out the names on wooded crosses they had made. He looked up at Tye. "These are the second and third that I've carved in two days. I hope they ain't any more."

"I suspect they will be corporal," Tye sighed. "We have an Apache that is madder than hell and I believe we will find out those two at the fort had something to do with it."

"I suspect so, Tye. What about the kid? We can't just leave him here."

Tye looked at Private Abernathy. "You've been on a lot of patrols in this area so I figure you could find your way back to Clark."

"You want someone to take the boy back, right" Tye nodded. Abernathy thought for a moment. "Yes sir, I can find the fort."

"I'll get him to get some of his things together and you two can be on your way." Tye went back into the house and sat on the bed beside the boy.

"You cannot stay here Robert. I'll have one of the men take you back to the fort. Later, you and I will come back up here and you can pay your respects to your parents. We'll keep coming back and keep this place in good shape and maybe one day, you can stay. I think that is what your ma and pa would like. How about it?"

Robert nodded and stood up. "I'll get some of my things." Tye nodded and went outside.

"The boy is getting some things together to take with him." He looked at Abernathy. "You two will have to ride double, but no more than he weighs, it shouldn't be a problem. Just head south private until you hit the Old Mail Road and then go east. You can make camp tonight and then be at the fort by noon tomorrow. I know you know this, but keep your fire small and try to find a place that isn't exposed too much." Robert came out of the house with two small bundles. One bundle held an extra pair of pants and two shits and some socks. The other held some biscuits and bacon his mother had made that morning. Tye took some and left enough for the boy and Abernathy to munch on. Tye lifted him up behind Abernathy. "Be careful, private." He looked at Robert. "I'll see you in a few days." He watched them as they rode off and then turned to the others. "Mount up. We've got an Apache to find."

Chapter Six

The soldiers had followed Tye for about two hours when the scout reined in Sandy.

"Why you stopping," Absher asked?

Tye pointed to the tracks on the ground. The Apache dismounted here and walked up the hill. Tye stepped off Sandy and followed the Apache's tracks. "You men wait here. Absher was trying hard to see what Tye had saw in the tracks, but wasn't having much luck.

To keep from being sky lined, Tye dropped into a crouch before he reached the crest of the hill. Peering over a thick sage he saw one dead man in the water, one half in and half out of the creek, and one that was propped up against a large rock. Tye could not tell if he was dead or alive.

Quickly backing down the hill, he filled the men on what he saw, and mounted Sandy. They rode over the hill and down where the dead men were. Tye quickly realized the man against the rock was alive. While Absher and the others checked the other two, Tye hurried over to the wounded man with his canteen. He was barely conscious as Tye poured some water into his mouth. Tye looked at the ugly wound above the man's knee and winced. He knew the man was in intense pain.

"You speak English," Tye asked?

"A …a little," the man mumbled.

"Who did this…who shot you and the others?"

"An…a Apache," he whispered. "Said his name was…Yahzie." Tye gave him some more water. "We were panning the creek and he came on his from nowhere. He shot Bill and Chance and then wounded me."

"Why didn't he kill you?"

"Wanted me to know his name and tell it to people. He said some men killed his family and he was going to kill every white and Mexican he came across…man, woman, or child."

"That explains some things," Tye mumbled under his breath.

"What do you mean?"

"Never mind," Tye said. "I'm going to make a travois and have you taken to Fort Clark. If that leg doesn't get some doctoring pretty quick, you'll lose it." He hollered at Absher, "See if you can find me a couple of strong limbs about eight or ten foot long. He walked back up the hill and down to where the Apache had dismounted. Circling the area he found his pony tracks leading north.

Returning to the man, he quickly got a couple of blankets and made the travois. He tied it behind Private Jacobson's horse. Jacobson was the only one beside Tye that could find his way back to Clark. He would take the wounded man to the hospital there and then report to Major Thurston. Tye told him to ask the major to figure out a way to hold the two men that reported this mess about the Apache until he returned.

"Let's hit the saddles," Tye said watching Jacobson leave with the injured man, "we're wasting daylight." The ground was soft here, not too many rocks, so the tracks were easy to see. Tye nudged Sandy into a gallop as he led the men north alternating between a gallop, canter, and a walk for the next three hours, stopping only once during that time to give the horses some water. Tye could tell by the tracks they were making up some time.

Tye had been doing some thinking during the last three hours. It was men like the ones back at the fort and their dead friends that keep the Apache stirred up. "*If it was up to me I'd soon see them and men like them hung. He knew though, that would not happen. You would never get a jury to hang a white man for killing an Apache.*" He shook his head. "*Maybe if those jurors could see what men like that cause, they'd feel a little different. A white woman stripped, raped, and killed is not a sight a man easily forgets. Lord know, I've seen it way to many times.*"

"*Watcha thinking Tye?*" Absher asked, reining his mount beside Sandy.

"Do What?"

"I could tell you were thinking about something and I thought I heard you mumbling under your breath."

"That obvious, huh?" Tye replied.

Absher nodded and smiled. Tye looked at the young Corporal.

"I was just thinking that men like those two at the fort and their friends that were killed are a whole lot of the reason the innocent men and women as well as a lot of soldiers are killed. If we had just let the Apache live his life and we live ours, we just might have gotten along with each other, but you have the Mexicans who put a bounty on

Apache scalps which resulted in a lot of Mexicans with long hair being killed and their scalps sold as Apache scalps. It didn't matter if the scalps were man, woman, or child. Then you have us, the United States Army, who has sent crooks in as agents on reservations who starve the ones who do try to get along with the white man. You have certain high ranking officers who believe the only good Indian is a dead one. They just don't have a chance in hell of surviving." They rode in silence for a minute before Absher spoke.

"You admire them don't you?" Tye put his palms on the pommel of his saddle and raised his butt off the saddle for a few seconds which felt good, and then settled back in the saddle.

"I guess I do. They have survived in this land for generations with only primitive tools and weapons. You put a group of white men out in this country with a knife and a bow and see how they would fare…poorly I would imagine. They have fought the Comanche, the Mexicans, the settlers, and now the army and they have managed to survive. The white hunters come in here a few years ago and just about wiped out the buffalo which was the Apache's main food source. All the different tribes across the country depended on the buffalo, not only for food and clothing, but they made tools from the bones. Even the bladders were scraped and cleaned and used to carry water. Nothing was wasted when they killed a buffalo. The white hunters took the tongues and skins and left everything else to rot, and yet, they have adapted. Yeah, I admire them for who they are and what they have done."

"They've massacred a lot of innocent people, Tye."

"If the Apache wipes out a patrol, or maybe a wagon train, it's called a massacre, but if the army wipes out a village killing men, women, and children, it's termed a great victory. There's something wrong with that."

Absher rubbed the back of his neck. "I guess I've never thought of it that
 way. You are right though, it doesn't make a lot of sense."

Tye nudged Sandy into a gallop. "We have an hour of daylight left so let's cover some ground."

~~

Dusk found Yaḥzie camped close to what the white man called Eagle's Nest, a narrow, deep, solid rock arroyo. Signs of many fires were all around him as this was a place a lot of his brothers had used for many years. He had found a small cave and retrieved some food from the cache there. The caves around the area like this one were used by the

Apache to store food and even weapons. They were the main reason the Apache could outlast the army on a chase because the army would run out of food and have to turn back.

After full dark, Yahzie sat quietly by the small fire. In the silence of the night, he felt he was not alone. Quickly looking around, he saw nothing and heard nothing. He softly began chanting an old song his father used to sing when they were around a fire like this one. Many stories were told around the fires; stories of how life was when the Apache roamed free; stories of Child-of-the Water, the Mescalero mystical slayer of their foes and of Killer-of-Enemies, his helper; and stories of Usan, the Creator. Usan created the Apache, gave them game to hunt and fruits to pick. He had created the Apache homes in the west. This was in the beginning and why the Apache would always have such an intense love for this land-it was theirs, given to them by Usan.

He fell into a restive sleep and a troublesome dream. In his dream, he was staring into the fire and was startled by an image of his father staring back from the flames. He woke up, sat up and nervously looked around before walking to his pony. Shaken by the image, he stood close to his mount and watched him closely. The pony was calmly munching the short grass; nothing or no one was near. He looked up at the black sky with its many stars and again was startled as a star raced across the sky. He had seen them before, but always for only an instant; this one was different, was visible much longer. He walked back to his blankets and lay down. He sat up again as he heard voices calling his name. He looked in the direction of the voice only to hear it from another direction.

"What is the meaning of these things? Am I having a vision?" He asked himself. *"That cannot be. Only chiefs, shaman, and great warriors have visions. I am not a chief or shaman..."* He paused for a moment. *"The Great Spirit Usan must be smiling on me. But what does it mean?*

Lying back down on his blanket, he fell into a deep sleep, and again dreamed. In the dream he saw his woman and his son. They were smiling at him, and in the next instant he saw her lying naked, her throat cut and his young son with his head bashed in. He saw many white men upside down. He woke up. He knew what the vision meant- the upside down white men were dead, killed by his hand. He felt an instant strength within himself. With Usan with him, he could not fail in his strife for vengeance. He want back to sleep, and slept soundly the rest of the night.

Chapter Seven

Dawn came and with it, heavy, low clouds that were below the tops of the hills. A ground fog added to the problems of Tye and the men with him. It was a chilly morning and the moisture of the fog made it even colder. Tye always hated this type of weather, not because of the temperature, but low visibility was a dangerous thing when in Apache country. Visibility was less than fifty yards.

"This situation gives me the shivers," Corporal Absher said, speaking to Tye in a low tone. "It's not the weather doing it either."

Tye smiled at the young corporal, his voice hiding his concern. "Just relax corporal. The tracks are plain to see and we are still three or four hours behind him."

"What about stumbling onto some more Apaches? Hell, I can't see more than forty yards or so."

"There's always that possibility, but its winter, and most of your Apaches are snug in their wickiup, lying beside their woman."

Tye had to laugh at the remark that came from the corporals lips. "I wish 1 was lying beside any woman instead of out here chasing a damn Apache, freezing my butt off, and can't see well enough to tell if I am going east or west or any other damn direction."

"Tye chuckled. "That's why you have me Absher. I won't let you get lost." The smile on Tye's face faded quickly as he turned his attention back to the trail. The damn fog seemed to be getting heavier.

~~

Zeb Cates entered Brackett at mid-morning and headed to the first saloon he saw. Jim, the owner, recognized him as a stranger and as was his custom, gave him the first drink on the house.

"Passing through or staying in our little town for awhile." Jim asked?

"Depends," Zeb replied downing the drink "Give me another shot." He laid two bits on the bar.

"Depends on what?"

"Looking for a fellow. You probably know him."

Jim, recognizing the southern accent, asked. "Who might this fellow be?"

"Big fellow, at least that's what I heard; he's a scout over at the fort. He goes by the name of Tye Watkins."

"What's your business with Tye?"

"Ain't none of your concern barkeep." He laid a dollar on the bar and took what was left of the bottle and walked to a table near the back wall. Jim scribbled a note and walked outside. He found a youngster and gave him a nickel to deliver it to Major Thurston.

~~

Yahzie had slept longer than normal and sitting up, he was surprised it was well past dawn. He almost jumped out of his skin when a voice spoke from behind him.

"We thought maybe you were dead my brother." Yahzie jumped up and whirled around, his knife already pulled from its sheath. He relaxed when he saw it was his friends Too-Shay, and Little Bear standing there, smiling.

"Too-Shay, Little Bear, what are you doing here?"

"Looking to help our friend, Yahzie."

"I told you I did not need your help back at the camp," Yahzie said, but he was really glad his friends were here. "How did you find me?"

"I followed your tracks and the bodies of the men you killed. I did not know if you knew soldiers, led by the scout Watkins is behind you."

Yahzie walked to his friend and put his hand on Too-Shay's shoulder. "I did not know this. How far are they behind me?"

"No more than half day-maybe a little less," Little Bear said.

"Come and sit with me. We will talk of the soldiers and Watkins."

~~

An hour after daylight, Tye stopped and stared at the ground.

"What is it Tye?" Absher asked.

"I think our friend has had a couple more of his friends join him. "Absher looked at the tracks. They looked like some unsolvable puzzle to him- just a jumble of tracks that he couldn't make heads or tails of. Both men dismounted and taking a knee, Tye showed him what he saw.

After Tye explained the tracks, Absher could see what he was talking about. "The two sets of tracks that are following Yahzie are about three hours old. One of the Apaches is a hell of a tracker. They were following Yahzie while it was dark, or maybe they just knew where he was going. Yazhie is four or so hours ahead of them making him less than a half day ahead of us. The good thing about the situation is that the terrain here pretty much dictates your path."

Private Carter hearing this spoke up. "If you know where he is going why don't we put our mounts at a gallop and close in on them and get this over with."

Tye smiled at the young private. "The reason I'm hesitating about doing that is the fog. If those Apache know we are following them they could have a nice little surprise for us. It wouldn't be hard to set a trap when the person you are trapping can't see worth a damn. Of course, if you want to hurry and get this thing over with, you just go right ahead and gallop after them. When we find you we will give you a nice burial," Tye chuckled.

Adam swallowed. "I'll go along with you." They stepped back into the saddle and headed out, Tye about twenty yards in front; about the distance the troops could keep him sight. Tye figured the fog would be gone by mid-morning. Until then, he would just pray they wouldn't stumble into a trap.

Like Tye had thought the fog had disappeared before midmorning, much to his relief and the men with him. The temperature seemed to rise as the fog lifted and it was now quite comfortable putting the men in a better mood. The pace was slow because of the ground had become rocky, and detours around deep draws in the terrain caused by runoffs from the rain over thousands of years. They came to the spot where Yahzie had camped.

Tye reined in Sandy and studied the tracks in front of him. "Damn," he muttered to himself.

"Anything wrong?" Absher asked reining his mount beside Tye.

"The two that were following Yahzie aren't following him any more."

"They've joined him?"

"That's what it looks like." Tye stood up and looked in the direction the tracks were headed. "I've got a gut feeling things are fixing to get interesting."

"If you are saying they are three Apaches we chasing instead of one, the word interesting is not one that I would use."

Tye chuckled. "You're right-dangerous is a more appropriate word I would say. Four of us and three of them-with the ability of the Apache I'd say that puts the odds in their favor."

"I'd say that ain't very damn funny," Absher blurted out. "How can you say that and laugh about it."

Tye mounted Sandy and twisted in the saddle looking at the two men behind them, privates Carter and Jacobson. "I believe our friend Yahzie, has been joined by two more of his friends. Take your rifles out, check them and keep them out and handy." He waited a moment for them to do as he asked. "Let's go."

~~

The trap was set and the bait was anxious to do his part in the killing of the soldiers. Yahzie was going to be the bait but Little Bear insisted he wanted to do it.

"You are better with a rifle than I," he had said to Yahzie. "Besides, it should be you that kills the scout, Watkins, not me or Too-Shay."

Yahzie agreed to allow his friend the honor of leading the soldiers into their trap. They had found the perfect place for the ambush. It was not obvious like a canyon would be. There was nothing that should raise their suspicion about a trap. The land appeared almost flat, but to each side of their trail was a draw that runs parallel to where he figured the soldiers would be. The soldiers would be no more than forty or fifty yards from where they would lay hidden. The cuts were about four feet deep with heavy brush along the top making it comfortable to stand and watch without being seen. Yahzie would be on one side and Too-Shay the other as Little Bear would allow himself to be chased by the soldiers and leading them into the trap. Yahzie checked his Henry to make sure it was fully loaded. Satisfied that all was ready, he smiled, anxious for the bluecoats to rush unknowing to their deaths.

Chapter Eight

Back at the fort hospital, Rebecca and the babies were doing so well that old sawbones said they may be released tomorrow. Buff had not left her side except when she was feeding the twins. He was becoming an expert at holding and rocking Ben and Nicole, something he never dreamed of doing. He would make little noises and contort his face trying to make them smile. Like Rebecca had told him; "Buff you are going to make a great grandpa." He hadn't believed her, but by damn, here he was and he was enjoying every minute of it. Mrs. O'Malley was his biggest supported and had filled him in on things that would be expected of him like changing soiled under clothes. She had turned her face away so he could not see her laugh after she had told him that. He wasn't so sure of that one duty however.

Major Thurston, reacting to Jim's note about the man with the southern drawl that was asking about Tye had sent two soldiers to escort him to post headquarter. If the man was up to no good, maybe he could dissuade him of his intentions.

A knock on his door interrupted his thoughts.

"What is it?"

The orderly opened his door.

"Sir, Private Abernathy just came in with an injured man."

"A soldier?"

"No sir. A civilian-a Mexican. He's unconscious." Thurston slid his chair back and standing up, rushed outside. Private Abernathy saluted.

"Sir, this Mexican was wounded by an Apache named Yahzie. His two friends were killed. He was sparred so he could tell everyone the Apache's name and that before he was through killing, everyone would know who he was. The Mexican also told Tye what this Yahzie had told him as to why he was doing what he was. Tye asked me to see if you could hold the two wounded men until he returned. He said he had a lot of question to ask them."

"Did Tye tell you what the man said?"

"No sir."

Thurston nodded and turned to his orderly. "Take the wounded man to the hospital."

"Yes sir."

Thurston turned back to Abernathy. "Go get some food and clean up, and then get some rest." He straightened up and saluted the young man. "Good job, private."

"Thank you sir. Am I excused, sir?" Thurston nodded, and watched the young soldier walk away heading toward the mess hall. Thurston walked back to his office thinking about the two men. *"I hope they are still in Brackett since they were released this morning from the hospital. I'll send a man to Brackett and if they are still there, have them brought back here to me. He wasn't sure what reason he had to hold them other than Tye's asking him too. Legally he could not hold them but..."* He hesitated as a thought struck and he smiled. *"Protective custody...that's it. It would be dangerous for them to leave until the man tracking them is apprehended.* He leaned back and folded his fingers behind his head, and chuckled. *"That was simple enough."*

~~

Little Bear sat on a high knoll watching for the bluecoats. He wanted to kill them as much a Yahzie. He had been upset when Yahzie insisted he wanted to track the white men down by himself. He lost his mother and Too-Shay a sister and brother. His thoughts were interrupted by movement on the horizon. He knew it was not the bluecoats he watched for because these riders were coming from the wrong direction. *"More bluecoats,"* he mused? He watched for several minutes, his eyes going from them back to the direction he expected the ones he was waiting for. The group of riders were still to far off to identify, but he did not think they were soldiers. They were not riding in a line like the bluecoats do, but whoever they were was coming straight at where he sat. From the amount of dust they were not walking their horses. He continued to watch until he saw who it was-more of his brother warriors from the village. He knew this because he recognized the horse leading the group-a magnificent paint ridden by his friend, Little Wolf.

He took his knife and holding it to where the sun reflected off the steel blade, flashed his friends. He watched as they immediately reined their ponies to a halt. A minute later, two approached the knoll he was on. When they were a hundred yards away he stood up and held his rifle over his head. One of the two rode back to where the other waited. Soon, all the braves were riding toward him.

He scrambled down the hill to where Little Wolf sat on his pony.

"Little Bear, it is good to see my friend," Little Wolf yelled when he recognized the brave coming down the hill.

"Good to see you too, Little Wolf."

Little Wolf looked around. "Where is Yahzie and To-Shay?"

Little Bear quickly explained what was going on.

"We will join our brothers and help with the trap," Little wolf said. He put his hand on Little Bear's shoulder. "Do not be foolish and let the bluecoats get so near to you that can shoot you." Little Bear nodded and headed back up the hill as the others rode away to join Yahzie and Too-Shay.

An hour later he saw the four riders coming toward him. Three wore blue uniforms and the other buckskins who he figured to be the scout, Watkins. He scrambled down the opposite side of the hill to his pony. He rode around the base of the hill and was surprised he faced the men who were no more than a hundred yards away. He expected them to be a lot farther. He fired a shot in their direction and wheeled his pony around and raced away-toward Yahzie and the others.

An over exuberant Jacobson hollered, "Lets the red bastard!"

"HOLD UP!" Tye shouted as the men kicked their mounts to chase the warriors. "Just hold up a damn minute."

"He's getting away. Tye," Carter yelled.

"We're not to rush after him till we see what's on the other side of that hill. Too many times, soldiers have fallen for that trick," Tye said.

"What trick?" Carter asked.

"Having soldiers chase one or two Apache and run headlong into a trap. We're not running hell bent for leather after him till we see what we're getting into." He nudged Sandy into a canter. Thirty seconds later he reined Sandy in. He saw the tracks of the ponies of Little Wolf and his men. "This is why you don't chase Apaches without knowing what's ahead." He pointed to the ground. "See those tracks. They are less than an hour old. The three we are chasing is now close to twenty."

"Sweet Jesus. What are we going to do?" Carter asked, desperation showing in his voice.

Lookee there," Jacobson pointing with his Sharps. The other three looked and saw the Apache; he was taunting them, prancing his pony back and forth and yelling what they figured was Apache words for some vile things.

"One thing for sure, we aren't chasing that Indian," Tye said.

"Just what are we going to do?" an excited Jacobson asked.

"Just calm down and relax and let me think this thing out." He quickly ran things over in his mind. *There's too many for the four of us to go after. That would be suicide. The smart thing to do is head back to the fort and report this to Thurston and let him put a large patrol in the field. Then again, in the time it takes to do that, more settlers are going to be killed.*

The dilemma was taken away without Tye having to make a decision.

"GOD HAVE MERCY-HERE THEY COME!!" screamed Jacobson.

"Don't panic." Tye said keeping his voice as calm as possible. He didn't need the men panicking. "Follow me." He led them at a gallop back the way they had come

"We need to go faster Tye-They're gaining on us." Carter hollered looking back and seeing the distance had closed considerably.

"Stay with me. We don't want to push the horses too much. Let them use up their ponies trying to catch up and when they get close, we'll still have some speed left in ours. They held their mounts at a gallop. Adam and Jacobson were looking over their shoulder more than they were watching where they were going. The Apaches were less than a half mile behind when a scream from Jacobson got Tye's attention. His horse had stepped in a hole and went down hard. Tye reined Sandy around. "Get your rifle and get up behind me quick," Tye yelled. Jacobson grabbed his Sharps and grabbing Tye's hand, jumped behind him.

Tye was glad to see that Absher and Carter didn't panic and keep on riding. They took off again, but now Tye was looking for a place to hole up. He knew, as strong as Sandy was, the big horse could not carry two men for long at this pace. He remembered a high knoll with some boulders on top that was maybe a half mile in front of them. They were riding side by side so all could hear what Tye said.

"The only chance we have is to fort up and hold out till a patrol arrives. Jacobson, you know this area. You can find the fort can't you?"

"Yes sir."

"I won't have time to repeat this when we reach that knoll yonder in front of us. Take your rifle and cartridges and give them to Carter when we get there. The three of us will dismount and fort up there. You take the horses and change mounts every couple miles and you should be there by midnight. Roust Thurston up and have him get a patrol back here quick. We'll try to hold them off till you get here. Understood?"

The young private nodded. "I'll be back."

They were reining their mounts in when Tye shouted. Carter, you and Absher grab the canteens, ammunition, and your rifles and follow me." Tye was already scrambling up the steep slope. It was probably fifty yards to the top but with the loose rocks and dirt, seemed a mile. When they reached the crest all three were spent. Tye looked and the Apaches were a couple hundred yards from the bottom of the hill screaming their heads off. They smelled blood and were closing in for the kill. Tye looked over his shoulder and Jacobson was almost out of sight. *"God's speed private,"* he mused.

"Get behind some cover and spread out. Carter, you watch the left side and rear of this damn hill. Absher, you have the right side and help with the rear. I'll handle the front with my repeater. Don't waste shots. Take you time and squeeze the trigger." Tye looked around and was surprised at the situation. He could have looked forever and not found a better place in a situation like this one. The top of the knoll was probably no more than twenty yards across with good cover. The slopes were steep enough that it would prevent a mounted charge and with the loose rocks, the Apache wouldn't be able to move quickly even on foot. Even with these things in their favor, he knew that it was only a matter of time before they were overrun. Tye, a survivor of countless fights with the Apache over the past fifteen years, knew one thing for sure: hell was racing toward them on painted ponies. He thought of Rebecca, and the possibility never holding her again. He thought of Little Ben and Nicole and the possibility of never seeing them again. These thoughts brought a lump to his throat.

"I'm not going to die out here in the middle of nowhere," he mused. *I am going to fight and kill the Apaches till the patrol arrives. I will live!"*

Chapter Nine

Back at Fort Clark, Zeb Cates was sitting across from Major Thurston in the major's office.

After a few pleasantries talking about the weather and the difference between this land and the place Cates came from the major asked.

"Mr. Cates, I would like to know two things: one, are you related to Yancey and Billy Cates and two, why do you want to see my Chief of Scouts, Tye Watkins?" Thurston knew if the answer to the first question was a yes, he knew what the answer to the second one was.

Cates mulled the questions over for a moment before answering. "Yancey and Billy were my nephews. As far as…"

Thurston butted in. "I figured as much and now you want to kill the man that brought your nephews in."

Cates did not reply so Thurston continued. "Do you know what your nephews did? Do you know anything about Watkins? I will tell you this, he did not kill Yancey. He brought the man in and I sentenced him to hang. Billy was shot at several times by Tye as well as several soldiers. He was hit four times. No one is sure who hit him." He paused, allowing time for Cates to say something before continuing.

"Your nephews, along with some of their friends, robbed the patrons of a saloon across the street. Several townspeople were shot and three died. Two of my men happen to walk in at the wrong time and were gunned down and both died. Later, after robbing and killing two families of settlers north of here they reached the junction of the Rio Pecos and the Rio Grande Rivers where they came upon a family building a home. They raped the girls, some of whom were barely in their teens, before killing them and the men. That is the type of men your nephews were Mr. Cates."

"Is that all?" Cates said standing up.

"NO, THAT IS NOT ALL! Now sit your ass back down before I lose my temper," Thurston yelled, slamming his fist on the desk.

Cates looked into the major's eyes and knew he wasn't kidding. He sat back down.

"Do you know anything about Tye Watkins, Mr. Cates?" Again, his question received no reply. "Let me fill you in on a few things you should know before you do what you think you should do. Watkins was born and raised out here in this land. He pa was a famous mountain man and he taught Tye everything about surviving this land which included fighting with knives, guns, fist, or any other weapon you can think of. He killed his first Apache when he was fourteen. He's thirty now so he has been fighting them for sixteen years. When he was with the Texas Mounted Rifles he tracked down so many outlaws they put a bounty on him. A lot tougher men than you have tried to collect-they are dead and he is still here. He is big medicine to the Apache and it would be a great honor to any warrior who killed him. He's still here Mr. Cates. People say he is as much Apache as the Apache are. I know for a fact he could kill you more ways than you could ever dream of. One more thing before you leave Mr. Cates-Watkins has saved every soldier on the fort's asses at least once and

Gary McMillan

they love him. If you did, by some miracle, kill him I can promise you every soldier on this fort will be after you. I would see to that. Dispatches would be sent out and the troops of other forts will be watching for you. I don't think you would make it out of Texas, Mr. Cates. You do what you want to do, though." Thurston stood up and reached to shake the man's hand. "It has been nice knowing you."

Cates stood up and shook the major's hand. "What does that mean-It's been nice knowing you?"

Thurston shrugged. "It just means, it was nice knowing you. I figure the next time I see you is when you are stretched out on the ground-deader than an old piece of wood. Now, if you will excuse me Mr. Cates, I have a pile of paper work to go through."

Cates stood up slowly, turned and walked out the door. He wasn't sure if he had been warned, threatened or just what the hell just happened. He was sure of one thing though; this might not be as easy a job as he figured.

~~

Tye watched as the Apaches', screaming their heads off, gathered at the bottom of the hill. *"Might as well start things off,"* Tye thought. He sighted in on the Apache

69

closest to the hill and squeezed the trigger. The Henry bucked slightly against his shoulder. An instant later, the warrior tumbled off the back of his pony. In the blink of the eye, the others were off their ponies and scrambling for cover. Tye fired a second time and a brave grabbed his shoulder and slid behind a large boulder. He heard the reports Carters and Absher's Sharps, but he was busy laying down a writhing field of fire at the Apaches coming up the hill. He only hit one more as they were doing what Apache's do best-show themselves for an instant as they moved up the slope and then drop out of sight before you can draw a bead on them. He drew his side arm and fired a coupe more shots just to keep them down while he put more forty-fours in the Henry.

"You two okay?" he hollered.

"Yo," Absher answered.

"Yo," Carter replied.

Tye figured he had ten or so warriors hidden on the slope in front of him. That would leave about ten divided up the other slopes.

"Absher, did you hit any?" Tye asked.

"One down and maybe one wounded."

"How about you, Carter?"

"Hit two, but don't know if they are dead are not."

"Good. We trimmed them down some. Now listen," Tye said. "They will show themselves for a second and dive for cover. They will be inching up the slope that way. Pick the closest one to you and sight in on the spot you saw him last. When he shows himself for that second, blast him to hell, and then pick the next one that's nearest you."

Both men acknowledged the order moved their rifles, sighting in on the last spot they saw an Apache-and waited. A minute went by, then two, and nothing moved. Sweat ran down each man's face, hands became clammy, but they did not dare remove their fingers from the triggers to wipe them. Waiting-waiting, that is the Apache way.

Suddenly with a shriek, about twenty warriors jumped up as one and moved a step up the hill before hitting the slope again. Three rifles cracked at the same time and three warriors would not move the next time. Each man sighted on another spot and waited.

"Nailed one," whispered Absher.

"Me too," Carter chimed in.

"Good shooting men-now get ready for the next move."

Yahzie looked beside him and then behind him, down the slope. He saw two of his brothers dead and one wounded. He figured some were dead on the other slopes too. These were warriors they were fighting and he did not want more of his men dying needlessly. They had the men trapped and could wait them out. He figured they had little food and water. He yelled a command in Apache and each warrior began inching their way back down the hill, staying below the tops of the sage and low cedars, out of sight from the soldiers.

"What are they doing?" Carter wondered out loud.

"Are they leaving-giving up?" Absher questioned.

"They're not leaving," Tye answered. "They know hey have us trapped on top. I'm sure they know we don't have much water and food so instead of losing more men, they will wait us out."

"That's just great, Tye. Thanks for making me feel better," Absher remarked.

Tye looked at both men and forced a smile. "You're welcome." He knew the three of them were in a fix, but he saw no need to panic them. "Take one swallow of water and eat a little jerky and then take one more swallow-no more. We have to make the water last as long as possible."

"When are you looking for Abernathy and the patrol to show up?" Carter asked.

"At the earliest, noon tomorrow, but more likely about mid-afternoon. We are in the fight of our lives and the only way for us to make it out is too watch each others back. There can be no sleeping-if you do, you just might be sleeping forever. Now, get that drink and eat a bit of jerky."

~~

Private Abernathy was well on his way back to Fort Clark. He was a good horseman and switched mounts without having to stop. The horses seem to be holding up. The only time he had stopped was at the Pecos-Rio Grande junction when he let the horses drink their fill and let them blow for ten minutes. He recognized several landmarks and decided he could save time by cutting across country, directly toward the fort instead of continuing south toward the Old Mail Road. He knew every minute he could save was important to his friends back on the hill. He pulled his hat lower on his head and nudged his mount into a little faster gallop.

~~

Back in Brackett, Zeb Cates was getting himself an education: not in reading and writing, but in what he was facing if he confronted this Watkins fellow. He was in

Jim's saloon playing cards. His playing partners were two soldiers, a trapper, and a Mexican that Zeb hadn't figured out just what he did for a living. The stakes were small, but he wasn't really concentrating on trying to win: he was listening to stories about Watkins from the two soldiers. Zeb had casually mentioned Watkins name in conversation and then asked the two men if they knew him. The two men took over the conversation after that.

Both men had been on the patrol when Tye brought in the fierce war chief, Lone Wolf. They described how the warrior had taunted Tye into a knife fight with all the men watching and how easily Tye had won the fight. They talked about the giant that was the bodyguard of an crooked Indian agent and Tye had whipped him in a fist fight not once, but twice. It was the only two fights the man had ever lost. Zeb bit his tongue when one of them related how Tye had beat the hell out of that sorry piece of horse shit outlaw, Yancey Cates.

After the story, Zeb casually asked what they knew about this Yancey fellow. Both men lost the good mood they were in. One spoke up.

"He and his bunch came in here one day and robbed all the men in here. Ended up killing a couple of them and then shot two of my fellow soldiers who happened to walk in at the wrong time. They killed several homesteaders for no damn reason other than to watch them die: killed the children too. Hell isn't bad enough for the like of him and his brother and the rest of that gang that rode with him. There's been a lot of bad-ass men come and go in this part of the world, but I'd rate Yancey right at the top.

The other man nodded his head and added. "I didn't see any tears when he was hung, but there was a lot of celebrating. Old Jim that owns this place was shot during the robbery and damn near died. He gave free beer to everyone after the hanging.

Zeb had heard enough. He said he had to go and one of the soldiers mentioned that they had enjoyed his company and stuck out his hand.

"I'm Langston and this character sitting here is Private Jed Pinkerton."

Zeb shook both soldiers' hands and turned to walk away. The private named Langston spoke up.

"Didn't catch your name mister?"

Zeb turned back and answered, "Zeb…Zeb Cates." The soldiers looked at each other before Pinkerton spoke.

"Any kin to Yancey and Billy?"

"Uncle." Zeb looked each of them in the eye for a few seconds each. "Looks like I may be seeing you two again." He turned to walk away.

"Just what the hell does that mean?" Langston asked grabbing the man's shoulder and turning him around.

As he was spun around by the troopers grabbing his shoulder, Zeb lashed out with his right fist. It caught the unsuspecting Langston on the chin with such force he was lifted off the wooden floor and back about five feet. Stunned, he tried to get up by Zeb was on him quickly with rights and lefts. Langston was on all fours when the final blow came: a vicious kick to the ribs. The trooper rolled over on his back, unconscious.

Pinkerton knelt over his friend and then stood up, facing the big man.

"You sonofabitch," he hollered and jumped Zeb, swinging rights and lefts at the taller man's head. Zeb blocked every blow with his forearms and when an opening came, smashed Pinkerton flush on the nose. The private staggered back, wiping his hand across his bloody nose. He looked at Cates, but with his eyes watering from the blow to the nose, he could not see him clearly. He waded back into the fray anyway. He shouldn't have.

Zeb, showing no mercy, beat the man severely with blows to the head and several to the body. The stomach blows were lifting the hundred-forty pound private's feet off the floor. Zeb would have beaten him to death if Jim, the saloons owner, had not stepped in with a pistol aimed at Zeb's head.

"THAT'S ENOUGH!!" he shouted cocking the gun. "You've won the fight. Now get the hell out of my saloon and don't come back.

"I'm going," Zeb said. His anger at what the men had said about his nephews and the fact a damn bar-keep got the drop on him made him say some things he knew later looking back, he shouldn't have said. I'm gonna kill you bar-keep for pulling that gun on me and I'll tell you something else: you tell that Watkins fellow that I'll be looking for him too. I'm going to kill him and take a lot of pleasure in doing so." He walked out the door.

Jim kneeled over the two men on the floor. Both were still alive but Pinkerton's pulse was weak-very weak. Jim, standing up, walked outside and found a group of men gathered wondering what was going on. He grabbed one of them he knew, a man named Walt.

"Walt, please go get the surgeon at the fort. Two soldiers are in bad shape inside…HURRY!"

Chapter Ten

The sun was setting and watching from on top of the hill, Tye knew it was going to be another spectacular Texas sunset. Every color in the rainbow, from black where the clouds were heaviest to blue where there were no clouds. In between the two colors were different shades of yellow, orange, and light to dark red. It was almost enough to make a man forget his troubles-but not in this case.

The Apaches had made no move toward the men since the initial attack. The men had not even seen an Apache.

"Tye, do you think they have left?" an anxious Private carter asked.

"They haven't left. Like I said earlier, they know we aren't going anywhere so they are taking their time. Just keep watching and don't get surprised."

"Man, I could use some coffee right now," Corporal Absher mumbled. "My eyelids feel like they weigh a ton apiece."

Tye knew what the corporal was talking about: he was about done in too. He hadn't had a good nights sleep since before they took Rebecca to the hospital and that had been three nights ago. He knew he had to do something to keep everyone awake.

"Absher, where were you born?"

"New York, in what was called the Five Point area."

"You're a damn Yankee?" Carter chuckled.

"I'm a damn Yankee you low life southern rebel," he answered laughing.

"You're a hell of a long ways from New York," Tye said. "How did you end up here?"

"That's a long story," Absher answered. "As a youngster, I was a member of the Dead Rabbits, one of the many gangs that roamed the Five Point section. There was a lot of blood shed between the gangs such as the one I was in and the Bowery Boys, the Roach Guards, the Blue Shirts and the Swamp Angels to name a few. Each gang had a certain territory that was theirs and if you, as a rival gang tread there, you were asking to get killed."

"Everyone was involved in crime one way or another: stealing, murder, prostitution, protection racket, or any other illegal thing you could think of. Not only that, but disease was everywhere. It was a miracle a boy could live long enough to become a man. Anyway, I got into some trouble and a kindly judge gave me the choice, prison or joining the army." He chuckled, "Right now I think I made a bad choice."

Tye laughed, "That story sounds a little familiar doesn't it Carter."

"You're sure as hell right about that, Tye." Carter had gotten himself into some trouble a couple months earlier when he robbed the rancher he worked for after being coerced into it by some so called friends. The rancher's wife and son had gotten killed in the robbery. After Carter saved Tye and Wallace's lives when he could have escaped influenced Major Thurston into giving him the same choice Absher had-go to prison or join the army.

"I heard some rumors to that fact about you," Absher said.

"It doesn't concern you that I was involved in something like that?" Carter asked.

"I can answer that for Absher and every other soldier at Clark." Tye said. "In this man's army a man's past doesn't matter to most. It's what you do now that counts, things like: being counted on to watch your buddy's back when things are tough-like right now. I know you will hold up your end of this fight and so does Absher. They are a lot of men in the army that have questionable past and enlisted to escape them. A lot of them are damn good soldiers."

Things were quite for a few minutes before Carter asked a question. "I heard that New York was over crowed with people."

Absher chuckled. "You might say that. I don't know for sure, but it wouldn't surprise me that the number of people living in New York was more than the whole State of Texas."

"Well, there are a lot of open spaces out here for sure," Carter replied.

"You cou…," Absher's reply was cut short by a curse from Carter followed immediately by the crack of a rifle. The brief flare from the rifle revealed several warriors only a few feet from their positions.

Tye started firing his repeater as fast as he could lever shells into the chamber, spraying the area in front of him from left to right and back again. Absher and Carter after firing their Sharps were firing their six shot Colt revolvers.

The Apaches didn't falter in the fevered rage to reach the hated bluecoats. They were almost over the crest of the hill. Chaos erupted in front of, behind, and to the side of Tye. Frenzied screams from the throats of the Apaches mixed with the gun shots and oaths from the soldiers.

An Apache came over the top at Tye swinging his war club down at Tye's head intending to smash the white man's skull. Tye, his rifle now empty of shells, blocked the downward thrust of the club with the barrel of his Henry. He quickly slid his right hand from the butt down the barrel to where his left hand was. Gripping the barrel with both hands he swung the Henry at the warrior like a long club hitting the man in the side of the head. The Apache fell at Tye's feet.

Tye pulled his Colt from his holster and shot a brave that was on top of Absher and firing again, hit one that was coming over the rim in front of Carter who was already grappling with another painted warrior. Afraid to shoot for fear of hitting his own man, Tye ran the four or five steps to them and brought the barrel of his three pound Colt down hard on the Indians skull. Carter gave Tye a nod of appreciation and then they were busy again with more coming over the boulders at them.

Tye shot one with his Colt, but the hammer fell on an empty chamber the second time he pulled the trigger. Tye thought he saw a grim on the Apache's face when the hammer fell and didn't fire. He dropped the Colt and grabbed his Bowie in his boot top just as the Apache dropped into a crouch in front of him.

Screeching, the Apache was on him, slashing with his knife trying to open up Tye's belly. Tye stepped back and sucked in his stomach as the tip of the blade raked across his leather shirt. The came together, each holding the other mans knife hand in a vise like grip knowing if they lost it, a knife blade would find its way into their body. They grapple for a few seconds each trying to gain an advantage. The Apache hooked a foot behind Tye's and pushed forward tripping the scout. Tye fell hard on his back but kept his grip on the man's knife hand and pulled the warrior down with him. The Apaches face was only inches from Tye's and he could feel the warrior's eyes, burning with hate, boring right through him.

Tye brought his knee up hard catching the man in the groin. With all his strength, Tye forced the hurting Apache over onto his back and using his strength and weight, drove the knife into the Apache's chest. Gasping for air he jumped to his feet and looked all around him. No Apaches could be seen-not standing anyway. Absher was struggling to get out from under a dead brave and Carter was sitting on a flat boulder holding a hand to his bloody head.

Tye pulled the dead Apache off Absher and helped the corporal to his feet. He was bleeding from a knife that was stuck in his shoulder. Tye helped him to the flat rock where Carter sat and looked at Carters wound. He had a big bump on the side of his head that was bleeding, probably from a blow with a club.

Looking around he counted five dead Apaches inside their little fortress. He knew there were more on the slopes outside of it. He looked back at his two friends and mused. *"With the shape we are in we won't be able to hold off another attack like that one."* He walked to the edge and looked down the slope. He could see three fires maybe a hundred and fifty yards away with several Apaches moving around in the dancing firelight. He looked back at the two soldiers sitting on the rock, hurting like hell. *"No matter what happens, I couldn't have asked for better men to be with,"* he thought. He walked over to the two men.

He took his kerchief and wrapped it around Carters head after pouring a little of their precious water on it, cleansing the wound.

"Thanks Tye. That feels a little better, and thanks for getting that damn Apache off me."

Tye smiled and patted him on the shoulder. "You're welcome private." He turned to see about Absher's wound. "This is going to hurt like hell Corporal, but it has to be done. He untied Absher's kerchief and rolled it up. "Bite down on this," he said handing it to the corporal. Absher clamped his teeth down and shut his eyes tight and nodded for Tye to do it. Tye placed his left hand on Absher's shoulder and gripped the knife with his right. He jerked hard and the knife came out. Absher's eyes flew open and he started to scream, but passed out. Tye laid his friend down on the flat rock. He picked up some small pieces of wood and started a small fire. He placed his Bowie's blade in the fire.

"Passing out was the best thing that could happen," he said.

"What are you going to do with the knife?" Carter questioned.

"I'm going to let the wound bleed a little more then sear it over with the hot blade. Bleeding will help clean it out some and the hot blade will sorter melt the flesh together sealing it." When he was through he put out the fire. "Do you think you can stay awake and help watch. I don't think they will try anything more tonight, but you never can figure an Apache."

Carter nodded. "We hurt them some didn't we?"

"I figure we killed about seven or eight so far and wounded a few more, how many, I don't know. They're licking their wounds right now, but don't go to thinking this is over because its not. He picked up the Apaches that were lying inside their little fortress and dropped them over the side of the hill, watching them roll a few feet before coming to rest against more boulders.

Carter spoke up as Tye took his position behind the boulder he had been behind earlier. "I always heard Apaches don't fight at night and wondered why."

"They believe if you are killed at night your spirit will roam n darkness forever. That's the reason for that idea of their not fighting after dark. If you are out here long enough though, one thing you will learn; you can never figure what an Apache is going to do.

Chapter Eleven

This morning promised to be a great day at Fort Clark. The post surgeon had just released Rebecca and the twins from the hospital and she, Mrs. O'Malley and Buff were walking slowly to Rebecca home. Mrs. O'Malley carried Nicole and Buff was holding on to the already feisty Little Ben. The old mountain man was becoming quite comfortable holding and caring for the babies, a far cry from a couple days ago when he was afraid to even try to hold them.

Mrs. O'Malley looking at Rebecca chuckling, "Old Buff's taking to this babying like a duck to water."

Rebecca put her hand on Buff's shoulder. "I knew he would. He's going to be as good a grandfather as he is at making a woman feel better by saying the right things.

Lord knows, he's done that enough times for me when I was worried about Tye."

Buff just kept on walking, smiling and letting Little Ben hold his index finger of his right hand. *They are right. I was scared about the grandfather thing, but it's working out. I never knew what I missed all these years. I sorter wish I had had some kids of my own now.* His thoughts drifted back almost forty-five years to a petite little Blackfoot maiden he stayed with one winter. This was before the Blackfoot became tired of seeing their game killed off by the influx of trappers coming into their land. *"If'n it hadn't been for the hard feelings that started that spring, I just might have married that little gal,* he mused. *"We might have had us a passel of young'uns. But, it didn't work out and now, all these years later I'm holding babies. The Lord sometimes works in mysterious ways.*

"You okay. Buff?" Mrs. O'Malley asked.

"Wh…what-oh yeah, I'm fine. I was just remembering something a whole lot of years ago."

"It must have been interesting because you was about to walk past the house," Mrs. O'Malley said laughing.

They all entered the house and laid the babies, who were asleep, in their beds. Buff poured each a cup of coffee and they sat down to relax awhile.

~~

Tye raised his head above the boulder he was behind to take a look below. It was a quick look because he had to duck quickly as a bullet ricocheted off the boulder. He looked over at Absher who was managing to sit up and watch the back slope even though he was hurting something fierce with the knife wound.

"He's like my pa said Absher's grandfather was, a tough old coot," Tye thought. His eyes drifted over to Carter. *"He's pretty damn tough himself. That blow to the head had to leave him with a terrific headache. If I had to be stuck with somebody in this situation, I could not have been better off with any one else. They'll both do to ride the river with."*

~~

Below the hill and out of sight of the white men, Yahzie was trying to figure out what to do. He wasn't so sure now about being able to kill the bluecoats on the hill. They were much better fighting men than he had expected especially the scout. He was a true warrior like he had heard.

He knew the fourth bluecoat had ridden to the fort to get help. They would be rushing to their friends to help them. "*Maybe they will not be so careful in their rush to help,*" he mused. He turned to his friend, Too-Shay.

"We will lose more brothers if we try to kill the bluecoats on the hill. I think more bluecoats will be hurrying to help them and they may not be so careful. We might be able to surprise them and kill them all. The ones on the hill cannot go far if we do because they are on foot. We can then kill them when they run out of food and water and have to come down or die.

Too-Shay nodded his agreement. "It is good. I will send Little Bear to see if he can find the bluecoats coming and what their path is. We can set a trap then." Yahzie nodded and Too-Shay left and found Little Bear. In less than two minutes, the young warrior was on his pony to find the bluecoats.

On top of the hill, Tye uttered an oath. "What is it?" Absher asked.

"They just sent a rider in the direction Abernathy went. I bet they know a patrol will be coming and they are going to set an ambush for them and there's not a damn thing we can do about it."

"Are you sure that's what they are planning? Carter questioned.

"One's not ever sure about what an Apache is going to do or not do. That's what I would do if I was in his shoes," Tye answered.

"You think that Apache is that smart?"

"Look at it this way, men. He has lost some men trying to get to us. He knows we're afoot and not going anywhere without horses, at least not far. On foot, in the open, we would be easy kills. He knows that the men coming from the fort will have one thing on their mind-saving their friends trapped on the hill. He figures they will not be careful in their hurry to get here."

They're going to ambush them," Absher said. Tye nodded.

"Damn them to hell," Carter uttered.

"I could be wrong but if that rider comes back and they all leave, you know that's the plan. Hopefully, Thurston found Dan and let his scout for them. He won't let them run into a trap." Two hours later, the rider returned. All three men were watching as the Apaches rode off.

"Damn," is all Tye could say.

"Lord, help them," Absher mumbled.

~~

Yahzie found a place that would be in the path of the soldiers. It was perfect. There was a four foot deep ditch made from runoffs on one side and the ground was soft here. On the opposite side from the ditch, they scooped out several shallow holes. Warriors lay in them with their rifles wrapped loosely in a blanket to keep the sand out. Other warriors covered them with a light layer of sand making those in the holes almost invisible. The warriors not in the holes scrambled to join Yahzie in the ditch. They waited.

Chapter Twelve

Major Thurston was worried. The patrol had left several hours ago and he had an inexperienced scout, Matt Schaffer, leading it. Tye's best scout, Dan August had left leading another patrol yesterday and wasn't due back until tomorrow. Tye had told him that Matt was pretty good, but he was young and inexperienced. He had Captain McClellan leading the patrol along with Sergeant's Christian and Arnold-all good men, but they were soldiers and not scouts. He was standing at the window in his office looking out on the parade ground, thinking, worrying. "Protect them Lord. Protect them."

~~

Matt was a hundred yards in front of the patrol. They were galloping their mounts trying to get to the men on the hill before it was tool late-if it wasn't already.

Abernathy was riding beside McClellan. "How much farther?"

Abernathy answered, yelling over the noise of the shod hooves striking the ground of thirty-three horses. "Maybe three miles, four at the most." McClellan nodded. He held his arm up and nudged his mount with his heels into a canter as the others followed.

A minute later, the scout reined his mount to a halt. He looked back at the patrol and when he did, he saw something that made his heart stop. Apaches were rising up from the earth and waving their blankets as they pulled their rifles from them. The blankets along with the Apaches war cries had some of the soldiers mounts bucking and uncontrollable. A few were thrown from their mounts, hitting the ground hard.

Rifles fired at point blank range ranked the soldiers ranks with devastating results. Screams of the wounded and dying along with the cracks of the Apache rifles mixed with the curses of the men trying to control their horses were deafening. The men thrown from their mounts had an Apache on them as soon as they hit the ground. Other

Apaches were pulling men off their mounts and bashing their heads with clubs or rifle butts.

Christian's horse went down and he came up with his Colt firing. Two Apaches were knocked backwards by the bullets from his revolver. Others were all over him in an instant. He cracked another's head in with the heavy Colt's barrel before a warrior grabbed his arm that was holding his pistol. He was choking another with his left hand when a war club split the back of his head.

Above all the noise and turmoil, the men heard McClellan scream. "Follow me," as he made a headlong dash toward the scout.

Matt had dismounted and firing the Henry given to him by Tye, was covering their retreat. Reaching the scout, McClellan had the remaining men form a skirmish line intending to ride back and help his men that were wounded or had been thrown from their mounts. He raised his arm, ready to give the order to charge when he noticed through all the dust and smoke that he could see no one moving- Apaches or soldiers. All he could see were blue clad bodies lying on the ground, not moving. He slowly lowered his arm.

"I wouldn't go back in there, Sir," Matt said. "Those men are dead and more will be if you go back." McClellan hesitated, looking around him.

"Where's Abernathy?"

"Back there with the men, Sir." Sergeant Arnold said, tears in his eyes. He had seen his best friend, Sergeant Christian, fall with several Apaches on him. He watched helplessly as his friend had gone down fighting with his last breath.

McClellan counted quickly the men around him. " Where's Sergeant Christian?

"Back there also, Sir." Arnold said, choking back his emotions.

"Damn," McClellan mumbled. He had thirty men counting himself and the scout and three extra horses for the men on the hill before the attack. He had lots of horses now, but twelve less men. Three of the men with him had wounds, but not bad enough to keep them from riding-just painful. He was always amazed at the Apache and the way they fought. They appeared from nowhere and like ghosts, disappeared in an instant. In less than a damn minute, he had lost twelve men. He shook his head in disgust.

"We are close to where Abernathy told me Tye and the men were, Sir," the scout said. "Shouldn't be more than a couple miles."

McClellan nodded and pumped his arm. The patrol set out at a gallop with several troopers holding the reins of the horses of those killed.

Tye saw the patrol coming and flashed the blade of his Bowie to get their attention. He watched as they veered slightly and headed his way. He helped the still woozy Carter down the hill. Absher made his own way, taking care not to move his arm anymore than necessary. The three men reached the bottom just as the patrol arrived.

Tye reached up and shook Matt's hand. "Good to see you, Matt."

Matt, smiling reached down and took Tye's hand. "Glad you are still standing Tye." Tye nodded and shook McClellan's hand.

"We thought we heard some shooting a few minutes ago," Tye said.

"They trapped us Tye. Gave us a real licking," McClellan replied. Tye looked at Matt and started to speak but McClellan spoke up.

"Don't blame Matt. Those devils were in holes covered by dirt. We never saw them till they rose up and fired point blank at us. I lost twelve men in less than a minute."

Tye looked down at the ground, picturing in his mind what happened. He had seen that before. "They come up screaming and waving their blankets?"

Matt answered the question. "Yes sir. They knew it would probably make some, if not all the horses go a little crazy and the men would be trying to stay in the saddle instead of fighting."

"I've seen it before," Tye said. Tye saw his friend Sergeant Arnold and looked for Sergeant Christian knowing they were seldom far apart. "Where's Christian?' he asked looking back at Arnold.

"Back there," Arnold said, his voice cracking.

Tye looked at their back trail. "You mean…" Arnold nodded. Tye bowed his head. Sergeant Christian had been a good friend and one hell of a soldier. Nothing was said for a full minute until he looked up at McClellan. "You up to finding some Apaches, Captain?"

"Waiting on you, Tye."

"Lets go back and take care of the dead first and we have some wounded that needs medical help." Tye, Carter, and Absher mounted the horses that were brought for them and the patrol headed back to where the ambush took place.

The Apaches had done what Apaches do after the soldiers rode away. The bodies of the soldiers were stripped of everything the warriors could use: guns, bullets, belts, knives, and tobacco. Every man was butchered beyond one's imagination except for one-Sergeant Christian. His body was untouched, the Apache sign of respect for a fighting man.

Tye picked up his friends lifeless body and carried it to a horse. He gently placed the sergeant's body across the saddle. He laid his hand on his friends shoulder and bowed his head and quietly prayed. "Lord, I don't know the relationship between you and my friend, but we both know he was a good man, a good soldier, and a man anyone would be proud to call a friend." He looked up at the sky. "I'm asking you, Sir, to take him home." Tears welled up in his eyes as he said. "Take him to Your bosom, Lord. He was my friend."

A minute later Tye walked over to McClellan.

"We need to send the dead and wounded back to Clark, Tye, but sending any men to escort them is going to throw us dangerously short of man power."

"Corporal Absher needs doctoring pretty bad. He can lead the wounded and take the dead back to the fort, Tye answered. "That leaves us with about seventeen or eighteen healthy men. I would guess that is about the same number the Apache have." Matt walked up to them. "How many warriors are left Matt?"

Matt did what Tye knew he always did when he was thinking, rubbed his chin with his index finger. "I'd say about twenty or so. A few of them may be wounded."

McClellan called the men over to where they stood and explained things.

"Corporal Absher will take you men that are wounded and also the dead back to Fort Clark. We will continue to track down the hostiles and end this killing." He looked around at the faces of the men. He saw determination in some, fear in others. "Any questions?" No one said anything. "Let's get moving then."

Chapter Thirteen

In battle, lessons can always be learned by even the most experienced warriors. Yahzie will never let a scout live again if he can help it. He felt like the stupid officer leading the soldiers would have charged back in if the scout had not been there. He had seen the soldiers lined up, ready to charge back when he saw the scout talking to the officer. He suspected the scout advised him not to go back.

The fight had gone as planned except he had not killed the scout and stupidly had not placed some men ahead of the soldiers to keep them from charging away from the trap. Even though all the soldiers were not killed his men felt his medicine was good-they had killed several soldiers, acquired more rifles, pistols, and bullets while only losing four men and having three wounded and of those, none seriously.

He had sent a runner, his friend Too-Shay, to tell of their fight to some of the Apache camps. He hoped others would follow his friend back and join his band. He stood on the crest of a hill beside his pony looking at the mountains in the distance. They were probably forty miles away and almost invisible through the blue haze that surrounded them. He stroked his pony's neck as he stared, thinking of his home, his woman and son, and how it was before. He thought of his father and grandfather and the stories they use to tell him. He was all ears as he listened to them tell of the old days when the Apache ruled this land and no one dared venture into it unless they had a death wish.

Listening, he envisioned himself leading his friends against the Comanche, the Mexicans, and even against the Black Seminoles who had settled the area south along the Rio Grande. He did not know where these strange people came from with their black skin, but he did know, at least he heard from his father, they were great warriors. He would never know these black Indians were actually descendants of run-a-way slaves who fled to Florida and were adopted by the Seminole tribe led by the great chief, Osceola. When Osceola was driven from the swamplands of Florida, his people were put on a reservation in Oklahoma. Some of the Black Seminole families escaped the reservation and traveled south settling in south Texas along the border of Mexico. They could not get along with the Apache and continually fought them.

Today, the whites were the Apache's greatest enemy. The Comanche seldom ventured this far south, the Mexicans for the most part were no danger to his people, and he had never seen the black Indian he had heard about. What he saw was the white man taking his land, the white soldiers killing his people, and taking the Apache's freedom. The Apache's way of life was disappearing before his eyes.

"What is my friend thinking?" Little Bear asked. Yahzie's friends' voice from behind him startled him.

"The old days-the old ways of our people," he replied. He sat down and Little Bear sat beside him. They both looked at the far off, blue hued mountains.

Little Bear was younger than his friend, but was battle tested, had counted coup, and was well thought of as a warrior like Yahzie was. Yahzie continued. "I am afraid the old ways are gone." He picked up some dirt and let it slowly sift from his hand to be blown away by the breeze. I think the Apache, like this sand blowing in the wind, will be gone soon." He was startled by his friends jumping to his feet and shouting.

"BEFORE THAT HAPPENS, WE WILL KILL EVERY WHITE MAN AND WOMAN IN THIS LAND. WE WILL KILL SOLDIERS UNTIL THE LAND IS RED WITH THEIR BLOOD."

Yahzie stood up quickly and placed his hand on his friends shoulder. "I agree with you," he said trying to calms Little Bear down. "We will kill as long as the blood pumps through our veins, but we must be careful in our plans. The white soldiers are like the stars, too many to count. We kill one and another takes his place. We are few. It takes years for one of our boys to grow and be able to replace a fallen warrior. We must be cunning like the fox, strong like the bear, and as vicious as the she-wolf protecting her young."

Little Bear nodded his head in agreement and sat down. "At first, with what you said about the Apaches way of life going away, I thought you had thoughts of surrendering to the white soldiers."

"That, my friend, will never happen. I long for the day the white soldiers leader is under my gun-I long for the day that the scout Watkins will be under my knife. The whites took everything from me, you, Too-Shay, and many of the men who ride with us. We will kill ten whites for every Apache that dies."

Little Bear explained loudly, "Not ten-we will kill ten times the number of my fingers for every Apache." The others were looking at him wondering what was going on. He sat back down.

Yahzie chuckled, "My friend is ready to do war?" Little Bear nodded. Yahzie looked at his friend in the eyes. "Then we will, but we have to plan every thing out so we do not lose warriors for no reason. We will wait until Too-Shay returns." Yahzie led his band towards the predetermined meeting place to wait for Too-Shay.

~~

This was Texas for you; cold one day, hot the next, and then cold again. Today, the sun was hot and the shimmering haze made distant objects distorted. Several lakes could be seen that were not lakes, only a distant flat rocky area. The men behind McClellan and Arnold rode with their heads down, tired and thirsty. Short breaks were taken to rest the horses. There was no thought of the men's needs nor was it expected. These men had been through this before when on patrol. When you were chasing Apaches you never saw them until they wanted you to. It was endless hours of boredom, sometimes followed by five minutes of sheer terror.

Riding across the arid, trackless land with parched throats the troops wondered about the sanity of the men and women coming to settle this land. But, come they did come looking for the free land they could call their own. For most, they had no idea of the hardships and dangers they were about to face.

Sergeant Arnold noticed the men were riding half asleep. McClellan smiled when the sergeant got their attention with some with some loud, stern language.

The patrol had covered several miles and had not gained much ground on the hostiles as darkness descended on the land. Camp was made and fires were quickly lit for coffee and to fry the bacon. Each trooper had one sourdough biscuit to dip in the grease to go along with the bacon. A feast for a king, if a man was hungry enough. The fires would be put out before full dark.

As the men hit the bedrolls, sentries were put out and silence settled in the camp. The only sound was the footfalls of the guards, the steady munching of the horses eating their corn, and the occasional melancholy howl of a lonely coyote. The men were too tired to pay attention and most were asleep in a few minutes.

Tye's bedroll was spread between Captain McClellan and his scout, Matt.

"Sorry about Sergeant Christian, Tye. I know he was a friend of yours," Matt said.

"He was a good man, a good soldier," Tye replied. "He was a man you could depend on when thing got crazy. When we get back, I'm going to see if I can find an address for his relatives and write them, tell them what a good man and soldier he was and they should be proud of him."

Tye and Matt both sat up as a coyote yelped close by. "What is it, what's the matter," McClellan asked.

"That last yelp weren't no coyote captain," Matt explained.

"Stay here Captain," Tye said as he and Matt threw back their blankets and stood up, both had their Henry's. "We're going to take a quick look around."

"Are you sure that wasn't a coyote?"

"Trust us captain," Tye said softly. "We've both heard plenty of coyotes before and we've heard Indians yelping like one. That last one was an Apache. Give us a few minutes to check things out."

Tye walked to the east side of the camp and Matt the west. They would circle the camp with one going clockwise and the other counter clock wise until they met.

Tye was startled by the crack of a rifle from the direction Matt had gone. He hustled back though the camp as men scrambled out of their bedrolls, throwing on boots and hats and generally wondering what the hell was going on. To a man though, they knew it was not good whatever it was.

As Tye ran by McClellan he told him to hold the men in tight and be ready for anything. The first thing he found was one of the sentries with his throat slashed. The second thing was Matt. He was sitting, leaning against a large boulder. Tye looked quickly around for hostiles. Seeing none he hurried over to his scout. He saw the feathered shaft of an arrow protruding from Matt's chest. He quickly kneeled and looking into the Matt's eyes, he realized his friend was dead.

At that instant, he heard the sound of a horse running away from the camp. He ran toward the sound and almost stumbled on the body of the Apache that either Matt or the sentry had shot. He figured it was Matt because the shot sounded more like a Henry than a Sharp which the guard carried.

"Captain. I need a couple men out here," he hollered just loud enough for McClellan to hear. He had the two men help him with the bodies and brought them back into camp. The men gathered around.

Tye pointed to the dead sentry. "This is what can happen out here if you don't stay alert. This man was knifed not twenty feet from where some of you were sleeping."

"Do I need to muster the men and chase the hostile," McClellan asked Tye.

"We can't track them in the dark. We'll be after him in the morning. Right now, we need to care for the dead and tighten the camp." Tye walked over to Matt and sat down beside him.

McClellan was giving orders. "Sergeant Arnold. Double the guard and bring the horses in closer and make damn sure they are hobbled and securely tied on a picket line. Those of you not on sentry duty or checking the horses, get some sleep."

The men headed to their bedrolls and one mumbled, "Fat chance of going to sleep after seeing Jones and the scout deader than a piece of wood."

McClellan walked over and sat down by Tye. "Sorry about Matt, Tye. He was a good man."

Tye nodded his head, lost in his thoughts. '*Two good friends killed today, Lieutenant Garrison a few weeks ago, my nephew almost beat to death, and I've damn near been killed no telling how many times in the last year or so. I can see where this Apache problem is going to end one day, but how man men, both red and white, are going to die before that time. I'm going to speak with Rebecca about the U.S. Marshal job when I get back. That sounds a lo…"*

"You okay, Tye?" McClellan said interrupting Tye's musing.

Tye answered without looking up. "I'm okay."

"Well, I'm sure as hell not," McClellan exclaimed. Tye looked over at the officer. "I've lost thirteen men today and one scout, and killed what, maybe four Apaches. A hell of a day I'd say."

"Men die out here, Captain. It's something you have to learn to accept. Men's been killing since Cain killed Able in the Bible. You ever heard of the Battle of Nueces or as some call it, the massacre at the Old Dutch Waterhole?"

"Vaguely. I think it was some Germans killed by Confederate troops."

Tye nodded. "It happened only a few miles from here. It's a perfect example of men killing men for no reason. It was in 1862, August I think. You had about sixty or so Germans from Fredericksburg and surrounding towns that was against slavery and headed for the safety of Mexico because they were ordered to leave by southern sympathizers. They were camped on the Old Dutch Waterhole, a branch of the Nueces River."

"They were attacked and most of them massacred during the night and still more that escaped were tracked down and killed. These men were leaving, not wanting any trouble, but were killed anyway. No one knows for sure who did the killing, but most think it was Confederate soldiers led by Major James M. Duff and a Lieutenant C.D. McCRae."

McClellan was wondering where in the world this story came from and why. "Why do you bring that up, Tye?"

"Dunno, Captain." It just popped into my head as another time that men died out here for no reason. Matt, Lieutenant Garrison, and Sergeant Christian, all good men, dead and for what? Because the men in charge, the politicians, think that with all the land we have, we still have to have the land the Apache call home. As a youngster, I grew up with Apache friends and saw how they really were. They are no different than us. They hunt, raise a few things to eat, love, have children just like we do. They do not lie and do not steal from each other. You sure as hell can't say that about the white man." He didn't say anymore for a moment. He looked at the captain and chuckled, "Haven't I said this to you before."

"More than once," McClellan said smiling.

"I feel better," Tye mumbled. "Just needed to get a few things off my chest. Let's get a little sleep." He lay down on his blanket, but sleep wouldn't come easy for the scout. He lay there looking up at the stars and listening to the night sounds which were interrupted every once in a while by one of the soldiers loud snores. He smiled when another trooper woke the guilty party up and told him to turn over in no uncertain terms.

If he did become a U.S. Marshall, he knew he would miss nights like this, camped with men who were good men, men one could trust, and men who would be there when you needed them. Course, they were not all like that. You had your slackers and you had men who would rather hide than fight, but for most, they were good, loyal men who respected the army and followed orders. He smiled again when he thought of the saloons in Brackettville. Every soldier he ever knew loved his beer. Very few of them had never spent a night in the guardhouse at one time or another. Even old O'Malley had done that and felt the wrath of the lovely Mrs. O'Malley. He almost laughed out loud when he remembers tha last time the old soldier faced his wife after a night at Jims. The six foot, two hundred plus pound man cowered before his five foot, one hundred pound wife's tongue lashing. With his last thoughts before drifting off, he wished he was with Rebecca and the kids. God, he loved them.

Tye woke up and looked at the stars to see about what time it was. One could tell by the position of the Big Dipper in relation to the North Star. He figured it was about midnight. He was wide awake so he got quietly up and walked to the edge of camp where one of the sentries was walking. He recognized the privates face from other patrols, but did not know his name.

"Having trouble sleeping Tye?" the sentry asked softly.

"Yeah," Tye answered in the same tone. "Lots of things going on and I'm trying to think ahead of what that Apache we are chasing might have up his sleeve." He stuck out his hand. "I know your face from a lot of patrols, but what's your name?"

"Garner…Private Garner," the soldier replied taking Tye's hand. He turned and begins marching the other direction staying on the perimeter of the camp.

Tye watched him walk away and then turn and come back. "I have seen you in action Garner and you are a hell of a soldier, but something bothers me a little."

"What's that, sir?"

"You look a little long in the tooth to be in the army."

Garner chuckled. "I'm old enough to be these youngsters pappy-hell maybe even some of theirs grandpa. I've been busted back to private more than once."

"Drunk and disorderly?"

Garner laughed. "A couple times and a couple times for hitting an officer."

"You hit an officer?"

"Shavetail smart-ass-know-it-all lieutenants that both times were going to get men killed. The only reason I'm still here in this man's army is because I was right and Major Anderson knew I was. He just demoted me from first sergeant to private-again."

"Where was this at?"

"Way up north, almost to the Red River at Fort Belknap. To keep me from being more trouble to him, he had me transferred here to Clark."

Tye was musing things over in his mind about this man. He would be a good one to keep the young troops from panicking in an Apache attack. "What did you do before the army?

"I was a deputy in Abilene and a couple other smaller towns. Had a wife and two girls. There are grown up now and living back east away from all this killing and robbing that's everywhere out here. I went back there for awhile with them, but it was just too damn peaceful for a man that was used to the life I lived. I still draw sergeants pay and send most of my pay back to them."

"Well, you go about your post Garner. By the way, I'm glad you're here at Clark."

"Thank you sir."

Tye headed back to his bedroll.

Chapter 14

The Apache leader was elated the next morning when his band found Too-Shay waiting for them at the place called Eagles Nest by the white man. Too-Shay had close to fifty warriors with him and there was much excitement in the camp when Yahzie rode in with his band. He hurried over to his friend.

"Where did you find so many?" He asked, looking around, amazed at the number of painted faces surrounding him.

"I only made two camps and when they heard about the killing of the bluecoats, I did not have to ask who wanted to come-they all were gathering their weapons and horses to come to you."

Yahzie looked at the faces of the men with Too-Shay. "They are young and untested."

"Yes, but they are eager to fight-to kill the white settlers and soldiers. I do not think the Apache have had this many warriors together in long time. With this many, we can kill many bluecoats and drive the invaders from our land."

Yahzie smiled at the excitement of Too-Shay, but he knew it would not be as easy as his friend thinks it will be. The bluecoats are many and they have more guns than the Apache, plus they have the scout Watkins that has always kept the soldiers out of trouble. That is the key he thought-capture or kill the scout and the rest would be easy prey.

"Come, sit with me and Little Bear. We will make plans."

~~

Tye had followed the Apaches horse from last night to the Apache camp. Reading sign, he figured they were three or four hours behind them. With the Apache knowing the soldiers were this close made Tye a little uncomfortable. All kinds of surprises could be waiting for him and McClellan with none of them making him happy. He stood beside Sandy, waiting on the captain and the patrol to catch up.

When they arrived the first thing McClellan wanted to know was how far behind they were. When Tye told him three, maybe fours hours, he was ecstatic.

"They know we are here captain, so it's not that all good of a thing to be this close. I suggest we take a thirty minute break to rest the horses and men plus they need to check their weapons."

McClellan cursed under his breath. He knew how Tye felt about keeping guns cleaned and ready to use. He should have seen to that before now. He gave the order to Sergeant Arnold to pass on to the men they would take a break and the men were use the time to clean their weapons after of course, taking care of their mounts.

Tye was honing his Bowie on a rock, thinking about Yahzie and what he might do. *"If I was in his place, I would head to Mexico and try to gather some more warriors from some of the camps that are located along the border. With the way the Apache thinks, after killing some bluecoats I would have big medicine and many should follow me. If I wanted the white man to remember my name, more warriors would help me to kill more soldiers."* He sheathed his Bowie and turned to McClellan.

"I think he will head to Mexico to get more braves. If he is determined to make a name for himself, he will need them. Killing a few civilians and twelve soldiers like he as so far isn't going to do it."

It was late afternoon and Tye and the patrol had covered almost forty miles when Tye reined Sandy to a halt at the place called Eagles Nest. He saw where the Apaches had been and was in total shock at what he saw. When McClellan arrived, he reined his mount in beside Sandy.

"You look like you have seen a ghost, Tye."

"Take a look and tell me what you see."

McClellan was an accomplished officer and leader, but reading sign was not one of his strengths. "A whole lot of tracks."

Tye dismounted and picked up a small limb and stuck it into some horse dung. It was pretty damn fresh-too fresh. "We've got a serious problem captain."

"What problem?"

" I'd say about seventy or so problems."

"What are you talking about?"

"Yahzie has just had about fifty or sixty more men join him."

"What!" Are you sure?"

Tye stood up and threw the stick down. "We're chasing upwards to sixty or so Apache now captain instead of twenty. Another problem we have is they were here less than two hours ago."

"Sixty or so Apaches," McClellan muttered to himself. He looked at Tye. "What do you think we need to do?"

"I think he will be hunting us pretty quick. I think they left here to go to the river to get water, do a little chanting and make medicine, and then come after us. You ask me what I think we should do," he said mounting Sandy. "Run like hell back to the fort while we can."

"Running like a scared rabbit galls me."

"We have eighteen men, captain. Yahzie has sixty or seventy men that ain't afraid to die. They will be more then we can handle in a fight. I don't like running either, but if we don't a lot more men could die."

McClellan hollered at Arnold, "Get the men mounted. We're moving out."

The men quickly mounted and followed McClellan. They immediately put their mounts at a gallop which surprised the men. The pace wasn't the only surprise, they had changed direction also. The more experienced men thought they were heading in the direction of the fort.

After twenty minutes they slowed to a canter and then a walk before galloping again. This was the scenario for the rest of the afternoon. At one brief stop to let the horses blow, Tye walked to a knoll with the field glasses. Looking at their back trail, he spotted a couple of dust clouds. They were too far away to tell if it was Apaches or just dust devils sweeping across the land.

Dusk found them still thirty or so miles from the safety of the fort. By now, each man knew where they were heading and why. Each time they stopped to give the horses a blow, they sat with their Sharps in their hands, eyes on the hills around them. There was very little talk.

"Do we make camp or keep moving?" McClellan asked Tye.

"I think we need to keep moving captain, but first, I'm going to backtrack a little and see if they are behind us. Tell the men to relax for a few minutes. I'm going to takes Matt's horse and let Sandy have a break. I should be back in thirty minutes or so.

Ten minutes after he left he was in trouble. He spotted some warriors about a half mile to his left coming in his direction. There was only twenty or so and he immediately knew what their plan was. The main body will be dogging the patrols tracks and two smaller groups will be a half to a mile on each side. When the main body makes contact with the bluecoats the other two groups will pinch in and hit them from the sides.

A few seconds after he spotted the group on the left he saw the main group coming from behind a hill no more than a quarter mile away. The war cries came immediately when they spotted the scout followed by their charging full speed toward their prey.

Tye wheeled his mount around and kicked his heels hard in the horse's flanks. He was lying low in the saddle, his hat pulled down on his forehead and his horse in an all out run back toward the patrol. Glancing over his left shoulder he saw the other group pinching in. He knew the group he saw earlier were now on his right was doing the same.

When he was less than a half mile from where the patrol waited he pulled his revolver and fired a couple of rounds hoping they would hear and be ready to move out when he appeared.

McClellan and the men heard the shots and were mounted when Tye came over the rise a hundred yards away. Tye blew into camp and sat his horse down on his haunches, stopping in a cloud of dust. He was off before his mount had come to a full halt and jumped into the saddle on Sandy. "Let's get the hell out of here," he screamed at McClellan.

They were off with Tye slightly in front keeping the men holding their mounts to a fast gallop. "They're gaining Tye," McClellan shouted.

"Just hold the pace captain," Tye shouted back. "Their ponies have been running all out for about two miles or more and they should be getting weary pretty quick. Tye looked back and saw that the main group of warriors was no more than a hundred and fifty yards behind them. The patrol no longer was in formation now, just running for their lives. The men in the back urged their mounts a little faster and when they pulled even with Tye he motioned for them to back off some. They did. Tye looked again and the Apaches where farther behind and slowing down.

"Thank God," he mumbled under his breath. He slowed the pace some. After five minutes he slowed the horses to a canter, then to a walk. Every damn man knew that he would be buzzard bait if Tye had not held them back. Their horses would have floundered and men on foot would be easy pickings for mounted Apaches.

The only sound as they moved through the darkness was the rattling of sabers and the occasional sound of a horse nickering..

McClellan took a deep breath and let it out slowly. "That was close, Tye," he said.

"Damn close, captain. Our butts are now out of it yet though."

"Why not? You saw their horses were exhausted."

"An Apache can cover forty miles a day on foot. If they a mind too, they could stay pretty close to us and hit us if we let our guard down. I'm not saying that's what they will do, but it's a possibility. I think its best we just keep heading toward Clark just as fast as we can get there."

Chapter 15

"Once again his plans had been spoiled by the scout. Yahzie stood with Little Bear and Too-Shay beside their lathered ponies, watching the bluecoats put distance between them.

Little Bear spoke. "We can stay close to them on foot and kill them when they break camp at daylight." Too-Shay nodded his agreement.

"No!" Yahzie said emphatically. "I know we could stay with them and possibly attack with the rising sun, but we will be close to the bluecoats fort, the place called Fort Clark. If more bluecoats show up and we are without our ponies…" he did not finish rather he let his two friends figure out what would happen.

After a moment, Little Bear spoke. "Yahzie is wise. We would be in trouble if more soldiers appeared."

Too-Shay nodded. "There will another day."

~~

Mid-morning found the men staring through red-rimmed eyes at Clark, no more than a half mile away. McClellan halted the patrol and had the men dust their tunics and hats, and make sure the dead were still tied secured to their mounts. They were tired, dirty, and thirsty, but they were alive. Right now, nothing looked better than the fort and hoisting a cold one at Jim's.

"By the two's men," McClellan shouted and pumped his arm. As they rode into Brackettville and on into the fort, at a quick glance, one would think they were on parade. No matter how tired and beat up, the patrols came back the way they left, sitting tall and in formation. Sometimes however, like this time, there were almost as many men lying across the saddles as there were sitting in them.

Tye and McClellan stopped at post headquarters and the men formed a line, facing them, standing beside their mounts. "Sergeant Arnold."

"Yes Sir."

"Tell the men,'well done', and then dismiss them." McClellan and Tye went into headquarters.

Gary McMillan

Sergeant Arnold turned and faced the men. "The captain said you ladies did well." There was some muffled laughter. "Now, take care of your mounts," he ordered, followed by a trooper's favorite word, "Dismissed!" The men shuffled off toward the stables. That cold beer would have to wait the hour or so it took them to feed, water, and brush their mounts, but there were no complaints. Each understood their lives depended on their horses and taking care of them was number one on any cavalry's man list of things to do whether he was on patrol or at the fort. The dead were taken care of and the wounded sent to see old sawbones at the post hospital.

Major Thurston met McClellan and Tye at the door to headquarters. He returned McClellan's salute and then shook both men's hands. "Come in. Tell me what happened. What's going on out there?"

"We lost some men, major. It could have been a lot worse though," McClellan said. "While following trooper Abernathy to where Tye, Corporal Absher, and Private Carter were holed up, we were ambushed. We managed to get through to Tye even though we lost several men."

"Where's Matt, your scout?"

"Dead major along with eleven troopers and Sergeant Christian."

"Christian...dead?"

"Yes sir, major," Tye said. "Sergeant Arnold said Christian's horse went down and the Apaches were all over him. He killed two, bashed ones skull in with his pistol, and was choking another when they over powered him."

"Sergeant Christian...dead." Thurston collapsed in his chair. "If there was a soldier that I thought couldn't be killed, it was him." He looked up the two men standing in front of his massive desk. "What other good news do you have?"

"After the ambush," McClellan replied, "We continued on to where Tye was holed up. We sent the wounded back here with Corporal Absher and Private Carter. We pursued the hostiles figuring there were only twenty or so."

"There were more?"

"Yes sir," Tye answered. "They were joined by fifty or so others. With sixty or seventy warriors, we were greatly under strength facing a possible encounter with a superior force. I thought the prudent thing to do was to come back, report the situation, and get more men. The captain and I discussed it and he agreed."

"I've never been one to run from a fight, but under the circumstance, I agree with your actions." He looked at Tye. "Where do you think they are now?"

"Attacking settlers. This is a pissed off bunch, major. They are going to do a lot of damage before this is over. I believe you can thank the two men who came here wounded and told the tale of their being trailed and their friends killed.
 one by one. Speaking of them, where are they?"

"In the guardhouse. Protective custody was the only charge I could think of to hold them on,"

"You did good major. Their friends and them two worthless pieces of horse dung, raped Yahzie's mother before they killed her and their son. I think they killed his mother or father also. That is why Yahzie was trailing them, why he is intent on killing a lot of other folks, and I don't blame him one damn bit."

Thurston nodded his understanding. "I will start the paperwork for troop of fifty men, plus your scout Dan, you, Captain McClellan, Lieutenant Lewis, along with Sergeants Hill, and Lambert." Both men nodded. "You can leave early in the morning. I will have a week of supplies for the men and horses, thirty rounds per man for the Sharps and thirty rounds for their side arms. The post surgeon will assign one of his assistants and an ambulance to go along." He stood up and returned the captain's salute and then shook both men's hands. Tye and McClellan turned to leave.

"Oh Tye, I almost forgot to tell you. You remember the Cates brothers?"

A flood of memories rushed into Tye's head…all bad. He remembered all the settlers, town folks, and soldiers those two killed plus Yancey's escape the day he was to be hanged and threatening Tye's wife, Rebecca. "How could I forget those two? Why do you bring them up?"

"You have a visitor wanting to meet you…a man by the name of Zeb Cates. He is the uncle of Yancey and Billy."

"What does he want?"

"Revenge. I enlightened him as to who he was wanting to kill and he might be biting off more than he could chew, but I'm not sure I convinced him. He's about your size, Tye, and looks like a man who as you would say, 'has been up the river and around the bend.' I think he could be a very dangerous man to tangle with. I wanted to hold him but you can't jail a man for what he says. Last I heard he was hanging around Jim's saloon."

"Thanks for the warning major. I'm going to freshen up, see my wife and two kids. I'll look him up later."

"You get some rest captain, and you be damn careful Tye. I'll have a man take care of your mounts. Now if you will excuse me, I've got a lot of paper work."

As they stepped out on the porch McClellan turned to Tye. "You want me to tag along when you go to Jim's?"

"No thanks captain, but thanks for the offer. I'll see you early in the morning."

Buff was sitting on the porch as Tye approached his home. When he got close enough to see the old trapper sitting in the shade he had to force himself to smile instead of breaking out in laughter. Buff, the old Indian fighter and trapper was so engrossed in holding one of the twins he did not even notice Tye until the scout spoke.

"What you got there old timer?"

Tye saw the old trapper stiffen. "Damn, Tye, I didn't see you coming." He stood up and stuck out one hand, holding the baby with the other. "Shor glad your back. Did you take care of the problem with the Apache?" he asked handing little Ben to Tye.

"Not hardly. That bunch went from twenty or so to sixty to seventy so we busted our butts back here. Twelve men plus my scout Matt Schaffer were killed in an ambush while they were coming to where I was holed up." He tickled Bens stomach and laughed when the baby broke into a laugh. "How's Rebecca and Nicole?"

"Just fine. Rebecca's getting her strength back and Nicole's a joy, just like Ben."

"Looks like you are getting into this grandpa thing," Tye chuckled.

"Never knew what I was missing all those years of wandering around trapping and scouting. I surely do wish now that I had settled down and had me a passel of kids."

Tye smiled. "Let's go in a surprise the lady of the house."

"Tye! What a wonderful surprise," Rebecca cried as they walked through the door and rushed into her husbands arms. After a moment, she stepped back.

"I know the routine by now," he chuckled. "I smell like a horse and if I'm climbing into bed with my wife later, I'd better take a bath."

Rebecca laughed. "I'll put some water on to heat if you will get a bucket full from the creek."

"I'll get the water from the creek," Buff chuckled. "We'll all be better off after you bathe."

"It can't be that bad," Tye said, and then laughed as Ben started crying.

"You're even too ripe for him," Buff snickered.

"I'll wash your clothes in the morning."

"I'll be leaving before daylight, honey."

"But you just got here."

'I know, but we have a real problem. We have sixty to seventy Apaches out there somewhere killing every white man, white woman and child they come across. I've got to help stop them and quickly."

"I know that," she said, tears rolling down her cheeks. "I knew the type man you were when I married you and that's why I love you the way I do.

Mid-afternoon found Tye walking through the doors at Jims.

"Howdy Jim," he said when he spotted his friend cleaning a table. Jim walked over to him, put his hand on Tye's shoulder and pushed him toward the bar.

"I need to talk to you-in private," he whispered. Tye bellied up to the bar as Jim walked around to the other side.

He leaned toward Tye and spoke softly. "The man sitting by himself at the table against the back wall has been looking for you. He's…"

"I know about him. The major informed me. He's why I'm here."

"Please don't bust my place up too bad," he said.

"Hopefully there won't be any trouble." He turned and walked toward the man. He was sizing him up as he approached him. *'The major didn't stretch things when he said he looked dangerous. He's big and built like a bull.'*

The big man had not looked up until Tye stood at the table.

"I hear you are looking for me."

The man looked up slowly, sizing the man talking to him up.' Depends on who you are."

"Tye Watkins," Tye said sitting down, but his right hand didn't stray far from his Colt.

The big man leaned back and pushed the bill of his hat up with his left hand. "So you're the big, bad bull of the woods around here."

Tye smiled. "Don't know about that, but I live here."

"Hear tell you pretty much beat up or kill anyone who you don't like."

Tye sensed being nice wasn't going to work. "Look Cates, I know why you are here so I'll speak my peace and then we will either part friends or step outside and settle this any way you want." He paused for a second to see if the man said anything. He didn't so he continued. "Your nephews were two of the meanest, sorriest pieces of shit I ever did see." The big man stiffened at the remark, but said nothing. "They killed for no reason-men, women and children. They raped two young girls and had their grandfather watch before they killed him. They killed several townspeople who were minding their own business right here in this saloon. They shot my friend Jim, who owns this place, twice. They killed two unarmed soldiers who walked in at the wrong time and then proceeded to kill two more families before we caught them."

'Billy was killed and Yancey was wounded when the patrol caught up with them. Yancey also had the foulest mouth of any man I have ever been around. He was put in the guardhouse and then sentenced to hang. He escaped by killing another soldier and made it be known he was going to kill me, but only after he had some fun with my wife. I beat the living hell out of him when I caught him. He was brought back and hung. He scooted the chair back away from the table. "Now you know. If you think those two are worth possibly your life, I'll be waiting outside, but I ain't waiting long. I've got a passel of Apaches to track."

Tye stood up and walked outside. He knew there were two types of men-those that talked a good fight and couldn't or wouldn't back that talk up or those that talked and would. He figured Zeb Cates was one of those that would. He sat on a bench just outside the door. Some of Jim's customers came out and stood in the street anticipating a fight. Zeb followed them out and seeing Tye, quickly sat down as Tye was standing up. He motioned for Tye to sit back down.

"I've done a lot of talking," he said. "I guess you are a man like me and know that I can't just ride away with my tail tucked between my legs."

Tye nodded. "I figured as much, but no one knows you out here and you have nothing to lose by riding away from this. No one back at your home would know."

"I would know, and that's something I can't live with. I've never backed down from anything in my life. I've heard from others besides you that Yancey and Billy were pretty sorry excuses for men, but blood's thick you know."

Tye nodded again and slowly stood up. "How's it going to be Cates-guns, knives, or fist?"

"I think fists," the big man mumbled. "Gonna teach you a lesson in front of your friends. I might just kill you later," he said smiling. Deep down he had his doubts as he sized Tye up. He figured all the stories he had been hearing just might be true. He stood up and took off his gun belt. Tye took off his and reached down and took his Bowie out of its sheath in his boot.

Both walked into the dusty street in front of the saloon. Tye took off the clean shirt he had just put on and pitched it to one of the men watching and telling the surprised man to hold it for him.

The two men faced each other and Zeb found himself looking at the most muscular man he had ever seen. He was looking at the scars. "Where did you get them scars?"

"Apaches-arrow, bullets, and knives. They have been trying to kill me for the last fifteen years." Zeb was sure he probably had bitten off more than he could chew and silently cursed himself for letting his mouth run. Tye said, "You gonna look or you going to fight?"

Zeb growled and swung a vicious right that barely missed as Tye stepped back. The right was followed by a left that Tye ducked under and as he ducked he planted a fist hard into Zeb's stomach. It wasn't soft flesh he hit, but felt like he had hit a piece of steel. Zeb barely flinched and caught Tye with a right as Tye raised up. Lights flashed across Tye's eyes for a second. The blow had stunned him. It was just about the hardest he had ever been hit.

Zeb knew he had hurt the so called invincible scout so he moved in for the kill-his mistake. Tye had not survived a hundred fist fights and countless attacks from Apaches by letting his guard down even after a blow like he had just taken. He caught the surprised attacker flush on the nose with a hard right that shattered the bone and gristle in Zeb's nose. A left followed so quick that it was almost like the two blows hit at the same time. The left caught the man high on the right cheek, splitting it open. Blood was freely running from the cut and from Zeb's nose. He was back-peddling trying to regain his senses when more blows rained down on him- hard blows to the face and even harder ones to his mid-section. He knew he was in trouble. Bending over, he covered his face with his arms as Tye pummeled him on the back with both fist. Zeb backed up quickly and stood up to face the scout who was breathing hard from the exertion.

Both men knew the other could hurt them. They circled each other, measuring their opponent. Zeb had his chin behind his right fist and his left was held a foot or so in front. Tye held both hands slightly in front of his chest, elbows in, protecting his midsection. Tye knew this man had been in many a fight and like him, had lost damn few if any. Zeb spit a wad of blood on the dusty street then wiped the blood from his face with his shirt sleeve. Both men were breathing hard.

Zeb moved in quickly, throwing punches left and right. Tye backpedaled, using his forearms and fist to block most of the blows as he waited for an opening. Zeb was tiring and he dropped his hands slightly. Tye put all he had left into a hard right that caught Cates just under the left eye which was followed by a left that was flush on an already broken nose. Zeb howled in pain and dropped to his knees. Tye stood over the man, waiting for him to get back up. When Zeb stood up the only thing that saved Tye was the years of living on the edge and having reflexes that was as quick as a rattlesnake's. When Zeb stood up he had a knife that had been hidden in his boot and his wild stab at Tye's stomach barely missed as the scout stepped back, raising his arms out of the way and sucking in his belly.

Shouts had gone up at the same time from the spectators which had become a large crowd. "Catch Tye!" Jim hollered as he tossed the scout his Bowie he had taken from the bench. Tye deftly caught it and smiled at Zeb.

"Couldn't keep it just a harmless fight could you Zeb."

Zeb didn't answer but charged Tye, swinging wildly while doing so. Tye stepped back as the blade flashed by, and then quickly stepped forward and planted another hard left. This one caught the former blacksmith on the chin and rocked him soundly. He staggered back a few steps, shaking his head trying to clear things up. Curses came from some of the men who were close by as blood sprayed on them as the big man shook his head.

"It's over Zeb. You're no hand at knife fighting and if you keep on, you're going get yourself killed," Tye said hoping the man would just give up.

Zeb stepped forward with a jab with the knife at Tye's head. Tye stepped aside, switching his knife quickly to his left hand. His right hand caught Zeb's knife hand between the elbow and the shoulder. He twisted the off balanced man around and quickly pulled Zeb's back against his chest. The Bowie in his left hand was touching Zeb's throat.

"Drop the damn knife, Cates. Drop it now," he screamed in the man's ear. "Drop it or die here in the street."

Zeb's knife hit the dusty street. Looking at the crowd, Tye spotted two soldiers, one of who was Private Garner. "Garner," he shouted. "Come over here with your buddy." When they came to where he stood he said. "Take this man to the post surgeon to fix him up and then take him to

Thurston. Tell the major what happened and I would like him to be held in the guard house until I leave on patrol in the morning. Ask him if he could place a 24 hour guard on my house with orders to shoot the sonofabitch if he gets within fifty yards of it or Rebecca. Understood?"

"Yes sir. I'll take care of it, Tye."

"Thanks," he said as the two left with the injured man.

Jim walked over as did some of the spectators. The one who had Tye's shirt handed it to him. Tye nodded his appreciation. As he slipped the shirt on, Jim spoke.

"You should have killed him, Tye. He sure as hell would have you. Now, you're going to have to deal with him again. I know his kind and he ain't leaving."

"Maybe a little time behind bars will give him time to contemplate the error of his ways," Tye replied. 'Maybe he will take a different path," he added with a smile.

"I doubt it," Jim said going back into his saloon mumbling something about Tye's sense of fairness was going to get him killed one day. Tye headed home.

Chapter Sixteen

As always when Tye was with his wife, time went by too quickly. An hour before dawn found him mounted on Sandy beside Captain McClellan listening to braying mules protesting being harnessed or loaded with pack saddles, noncoms course language bellowing orders, and troopers cursing while loading the wagon and ambulance. First Lieutenant Baker, and Second Lieutenants Lewis and Jefferson, two line sergeants, a first sergeant, a trumpeter, two Farriers, three corporals, and sixty troopers joined Tye and McClellan making up the column. Private Adam Carter, recovered from his head wound, was included as was Private Garner. It was one of the largest troops of soldiers ever assembled at Clark for a campaign.

Each man was issued thirty rounds for his Sharps and a full belt for his side arm. The U.S. Flag and the guidon of A, B and F troops flapped nosily in the brisk, early morning breeze. Sitting tall in the McClellan saddle, the men rode two abreast over the bridge over Los Moras and swung west on the Old Mail Road. A few townspeople that were up this early heard the sound of hooves striking the wooden planks of the bridge and quit what they were doing to watch, wondering what was going on. They were used to seeing patrols of twelve or fifteen men, but not a troop of seventy or so men, several pack mules and an army ambulance.

Tye rode beside McClellan and would do so until later when they would leave the road. Then, he would then take his usual lonely position a quarter or so mile in front, looking for sign of the hostiles.

~~

Many miles to the north and west of where the patrol rode, Yahzie was alone, high on a cliff overlooking the Rio Grande. He had eaten nothing or dank anything in many hours. He had come to this place seeking a vision, hoping the gods would endow him with strength and wisdom to lead his people to victory.

Apaches, like most Native Americans, viewed success in life as a gift from the gods. Seeking this gift, many Indians have taken solitary journeys to remote locations where in fasting, they prayed in hope of receiving divine guidance.

Even though visions were big medicine to all tribes the young warriors riding with Yahzie were impatient-they wanted to kill more whites. With their numbers they felt they could not be stopped and even thought more of their friends may come to them. Most thought they should be killing the invaders, not waiting on their leader to receive a vision.

~~

A few hours and many miles later, the troops were not sitting so tall. They had settled into the routine of most patrols-riding slumped in the saddle and half asleep. That was what came from boring hours and days of chasing an enemy that you would never see until he wanted you too. Dry throats, heat, boredom, and the endless miles of arid terrain was an enemy that could be as dangerous as the Apache.

A break was taken at mid-afternoon and Tye was sitting with Captain McClellan, First lieutenant Baker and Second Lieutenants, Jefferson and Lewis. Tye had not been on patrol with the lieutenants as each had been recently assigned to Fort Clark. He decided now was as good a time as any to talk with them, get to know them a little. He knew they would be dependable in a fight because he had never seen a Point grad that wasn't. At least he had never seen one shot in the back running away. First Lieutenant Baker had previous experience with the Apache at another fort, but he knew Lewis and Jefferson had not.

"Both of you men are new out here," he said, "And there are a few hundred things you need to know, but most of them will come with experience-if you live long enough." McClellan had to try hard to keep from smiling. He had heard this before from Tye, but he knew it was being told to them to help them just as it had him.

"I know you have heard of the Fetterman massacre back in '66." Both men nodded their heads as Tye continued. "Fetterman was a pompous ass who had no respect for the Indian. He felt he could take eighty men and ride through the whole Sioux nation. I've seen a lot of young lieutenants come out here who knew all that was to be learned from the books on how to fight a war. I'm here to tell you, and Captain McClellan will verify this, you can forget ninety per cent of that shit you learned at the point. It's all different out here fighting the Apache. You will see on this patrol what I am talking about. You might just get lucky and not even see an Apache on this patrol." Lewis spoke up.

"Why would you say we would be lucky."

"Because you would live to go on another patrol. The Apache fight a hit a run war. They are not going to face the army in the open because they don't have the men to lose in a battle like that. You may go for days without seeing one and then they hit you, kill a few men, and then will be gone and you are wondering what the hell happened. I mentioned Fetterman because he supposedly fell for the oldest trick the Indians use. They will show you a few braves. Get you to chase them and then the main bunch will ambush you and you're history."

"The best advice I can give you is to listen to the men who have been out here for awhile especially the line sergeants that will be with you. They have seen just about everything the Apache can throw at you and if you listen, you might live to fight another day. Remember this, while you were young and chasing girls, a young Apache boy was learning to track, read sign, and fight. At sixteen or so he would have probably killed his first enemy and by the time he is your age around twenty or so, he is a veteran of countless fights and killed many of his people's enemies.

Don't under estimate him just because he has no education like you. His education has been one of survival and he is damn good at it."

" Learn the lay of the land and especially where the water holes and springs are. Don't be afraid to ask me or McClellan a question, no matter how dumb you may think it is. Keep your eyes and ears open, ask questions, and think things out before you give an order and you might just make it out here." He stood up and walked over to Sandy, mounted and rode off.

McClellan nodded. "Sergeant Arnold," he shouted.

"Sir," Arnold said standing up.

"Have the men prepare to move out."

"Yes sir." He turned to the bugler and ordered him to blow 'Boots and Saddles'. The troop was quickly formed and headed out, following Tye who was shaking his head, chuckling.

"Damn army and its bugle calls, creaking wagons, saddles, and rattling sabers. Every damn Apache within a mile knows we are coming and where we are twenty-four hours a day." He patted Sandy on the neck, "Time we went to work and earned our pay old boy," he said and then smiled when Sandy nickered.

McClellan tuned in the saddle and told First Sergeant Arnold to have Lieutenants Jefferson and Lewis come to the head of the column. When they arrived, one rode on each side of the captain.

"Just thought I would follow up on some of the things Tye said earlier that might just save you and your men's lives some day. What he said about the Apache trick of getting an officer to chase a few braves and then ambush them happened to me. About a year ago I was leading a patrol and Tye was way out front scouting like he is now. Three Apache braves showed themselves and were shouting in Apache lingo what were probably insults at us. Despite my first sergeant yelling me not to, I led the men after the three. A mile later we were fighting for our lives as we ran headlong into a whole passel of waiting Apaches. All of us would have been killed if Tye had not come and got us out. As it was, my enthusiasm got several men killed and wounded. I was pretty upset at myself and figured my career was over, but Tye talked to me and explained a few things. He asked me if I ever thought that no one under my command would ever die. Men dying are part of war and he had plenty die under his command when he was with the Rangers. It's something, although not pleasant, was just the way it was and always will be as long as there was a war to fight."

"He did not report my stupidity to Major Thurston. That's the type of man he is. He knows men make mistakes and he only gets upset if you make the same one twice. When you are in the field leading a patrol listen to Tye if he is with you or one of the other scouts, First Sergeant Arnold, Master Sergeant O'Malley, your line sergeants, and officers like me who have been in the field awhile and you as Tye would say, just might make it out here. Now get back to your troops." Both men saluted, whirled their mounts around and trotted back to their men. McClellan mumbled, "Feels good to be able to tell men like them things that might save them some day. Not all are as lucky as I was and get a second chance." He smiled.

Tye was kneeling on the ground studying fresh tracks. He stood up beside Sandy and scratched the horse under the chin while staring off in the distance. "Looks like more settlers, Sandy. More people not knowing what they are getting into by coming out here." He heard the patrol coming and looked over his shoulder. They were still a quarter mile away, but one could hear the noise clearly. The scout shook his head and waited.

McClellan raised his arm and the troops halted. "You find something?" he asked Tye as he dismounted and handed his mounts reins to a trooper.

"Settlers, sir," he said nodding toward the wagon tracks. "Looks like three wagons. He pointed to some other tracks. Looks like they have some cows tied behind the wagons and some hogs are trailing them also. They're probably three families traveling together for safety or maybe all one family. Whatever, they are heading toward where I figure the Apache are."

"How old are the tracks?"

"Maybe ten hours, give or take a couple."

"Shit," McClellan spit out. Tye smiled in spite of the situation because the captain never cursed. Both knew they were too far behind to help the people if the Apaches found them, which they surely would because tracks of heavy wagons would stay for several days.

Tye mounted Sandy and was looking west, the direction the wagons were headed, when he saw the lone rider.

"Apache sir," he said pointing with his Henry toward the rider who sat looking toward then.

McClellan saw the rider but could not tell if it was an Apache, soldiers, or civilian. He took his field glasses from his saddle bag and looked at the rider. It was an Indian alright. He handed them to Tye.

"It's an Apache sir, like I said." As he spoke the warrior turned and rode away.

"What do you make of it?" McClellan asked still wondering how in heavens name Tye knew for certain it was an Apache from the time he saw him.

"Dunno for sure, but one thing's for sure."

"What's that?"

"We won't be surprising them. I'll go see if I can stir them up some and lead them to you," he said smiling and whirled Sandy around and headed west, toward who knows what kind of trouble.

Chapter Seventeen

Sitting on the bench seat of their wagons with their wives, the three men stared at the valley below them. It had been a long trip from their home in Missouri and looking at the valley, each knew their search for a place to settle was over. After stepping down from the wagons and kneeling for a prayer of thankfulness, they stepped back up in their wagons and began moving slowly down the slope to what they hoped would be their new home.

The valley was almost a half mile wide at the widest point and less than a quarter mile at the narrowest. It appeared to be over a mile long, more than enough land for three families. They could not believe no one had claimed this land and it bothered Jim Burgess, the oldest of the three men.

"Oh my God! Alice Burgess screamed as she saw the Apaches on the rim of the canyon to their left.. Her husband stopped the little caravan beside a small four foot deep ravine that had been cut by the run-off of rain from the canyon rims over thousands of years. He placed his wife and two small children, a boy seven and a girl five, in the bottom of the ravine. Her brothers had their wives there also. Neither of them had any children. The wives were given pistols. They had discussed the possibility of it coming to this and had gone over what they were to do. They would save the last bullet for themselves. The children had been well versed in not showing fear if the Indians came. Somewhere they had heard that Indians were kind to children and if they were not whimpering and showed no fear, they would probably take them and raise them to be Apache. They thought that was better than being dead.

The men took their positions with their rifles. Each had a Henry and plenty of ammunition. They waited. Alice sat with her back against the rock wall of the ravine with her arms around her two children.

"Why don't they attack?" Les the youngest of the brothers asked.

"I don't figure they are in any hurry," Brad said. "They're damn sure we ain't going anywhere anytime soon."

"I always heard that Apaches run in small groups," Les, the youngest said, his quivering voice betraying his fear. "God, they must be fifty of them."

"Just stay calm, Les," Brad said. There are not fifty Apaches, more like twenty or thirty. We're all good shots and with these Henry's we can throw a lot lead at them devils- maybe discourage them some."

Jim Burgess shook his head at his wives two brother's remarks. He had fought Indians before and knew they would attack when they were sure it was to their advantage. With fairly open ground all around and with them being in the ravine and well protected, the Indians would not want to lose a lot of men unnecessarily. He knew they were in big trouble and he cursed himself for talking his wife into coming out here and bringing her brothers and their wives with them. He was certain they were going to die-either today or tomorrow, but death was a sure thing. Three men facing ten to one odds is not a good situation. He looked at the sun and figured they had about an hour of good light left. If the Apaches did not attack before dark, he knew it was going to be one long night, probably his, his wife's, and her brothers last night on this earth.

~~

There was to be a full moon tonight and very few clouds which prompted McClellan to ask Tye what he thought about a forced march until midnight. He and Tye were drinking coffee discussing the situation. The men figured they were camped for the night, but McClellan had other ideas.

"I cant' get the thought of what will happen to those people in the wagons," he said, concern showing in his voice.

Tye took a sip of the hot coffee. "I know, but there are a lot of others out there that's going to feel this Apache's wrath too."

"What do you think about keeping on going for a few hours? There will be a full moon and few clouds," the captain said, looking up at the sky.

Tye stood up and threw the remaining coffee into the fire resulting in sparks flying. "You're running the show captain. If that's what you want then let's do it, but you can tell the men, not me," he added with a smile.

An hour later they had traveled about five miles and it was becoming dark. Tye had been right in that the men weren't too happy with their captain. McClellan called a halt, figuring to wait until the moon was up so they could see a little better. He wasn't going to lose any horses or men being injured riding in the dark.

Private Garner sat beside First Sergeant Arnold and the two line sergeants, Hill and Lambert. Arnold knew Garner's background of being a top soldier and of his being busted many times in rank. Garner's always being promoted back to first sergeant after being busted spoke volumes of what his superiors thought of him. He also knew that Hill and Lambert were good soldiers, but they were new as far as being line sergeants.

"Garner, what do you think the responsibilities of a top line sergeant are?" He winked at Garner when the old soldier looked at him. Garner knew what Arnold wanted him to say.

"I'd say putting their men first. You are their teacher, and you are responsible for them twenty-four hours a day. You teach them everything they need to know to stay alive and especially the importance of taking care of their mounts. Teach them to follow orders as if it was God himself giving them. As a line sergeant the men under you will look to you when the Apache are screaming and bullets and arrows are flying everywhere. You mess up and a lot of men are going to die."

"Well said Mr. Garner. I could not have said it better myself. Remember what he said you two and you might just live long enough to make first sergeant some day."

"We'll remember," Hill said. "This patrol has been an educational experience for both of us. Tye gave a long speech to Second Lieutenant Lewis earlier, but I think it was for our benefit also."

Arnold looked each man in the eye before speaking. "There's one thing for sure in this world-whatever that scout says, you listen, because no one knows this land or the Apache better than he does. The good thing about Tye is that even though he's the best and probably knows it, he never lets it go to his head. He will help anyone who asks him for help. He would lay down his life for a friend and I can say that from first hand experience. He…" he was interrupted by the order to mount up. There was some grumbling among the men who thought they would be making camp this time, but Hill and Lambert jumped them with a stern voice mingled with some four letter words that made Arnold proud of the two of them. Garner looked at him and smiled.

The moon was up and the landscape took on its glow. With the moonlight, white boulders stood out from the much darker ground. The light was enough to cast shadows of the men and horses as they moved along following Tye. Tye had never like scouting on nights like this. There was enough light to be accurate with a rifle at a fairly long range and he always felt like he was in an Apaches sights, but he wasn't in command so as he rode, he was even more alert than usual.

~~

Yahzie was still sitting on the crest of the hill, waiting for Usen, the life giver, to show him a vision. As if in a trance he slowly swayed his upper body to a long forgotten song that was in his head and would not go away. The song had been sung to him by his grandfather many years ago. It told of the old ways, chasing buffalo and deer, of raiding the Comanche for horses and slaves, of living a carefree life, free to go and come as one wished. It was a song known only to his grandfather and to him. His grandfather had told Yahzie stories his grandfather had passed to him. They were stories of the Apache coming from the north to settle in this land. There were stories of the early Spaniards coming into their land with their horses and shiny metal suits looking for the yellow rock found in the ground that was so important to them. Many battles between them and the people occurred over the next few years until the Spaniards left.

Before leaving, they had built several beautiful buildings they called missions and tried to convert the Apache to their faith. The only good thing coming from the Spaniards, Yahzie's great, great grandfather said, was the horse. The horse completely change the Apache way of life.

Yahzie's head was spinning, his body moving with a mind of its own and he was now chanting some unknown song to his friend's ears who watched from a distance. It was obvious to Little Bear and Too-Shay something was happening as they watched and listened to their friend. As they watched, Yahzie slowly stood, and with his eyes closed stretched his arms above him toward the sky. He slowly raised his head until his face also faced the sky. His body began to shake as one does with a fever. Sweat poured from his body even though it was early morning and still dark. A language unknown to them came from Yahzie's mouth. His body began shaking violently just before he collapsed to the ground. Too-Shay and Little Bear rushed to him, picked him up and carried him to a blanket under a large cedar.

Laying him down, they poured water on his face and a little in his mouth. He appeared to be sleeping, but the water on his face had no affect on his condition.

"Place a blanket under his head and we will watch him for awhile," Little Bear said. Just as the words came from his mouth, their friend's eyes suddenly opened. Yahzie sat up, swayed a little as if he was drunk. He grasped the gourd holding the water and drank deeply.

"What did you see?" An excited Too-Shay asked.

"Yes, tell us what you saw-what you heard," Little Bear begged.

"Soldiers, many dead bluecoats lying on the ground. Wagons of men, women, and children leaving our land."

"Did you see how this great deed will be done?"

Yahzie smiled. "Yes. I will tell you after I eat and sleep." He looked around. "Where are the others?"

"They did not want to wait for you. They went to kill soldiers." Yahzie did not answer. He shrugged, lay down on a blanket and was immediately asleep.

Chapter Eighteen

The night had been long just as Jim Burgess had figured it would be. The sun would be rising over the crest of the hill within an hour. He thought the Apaches would come with the sun at their back. He gathered everyone around him. "I think they will come just as the sun shows itself over the crest of that rim yonder," he said pointing with his Henry. "Honey, you and your sisters sit with your backs against this wall with the kids. It's going to get loud and nasty so don't panic and start to run or anything like that. We have a lot of firepower and might just kill enough of them to discourage them from losing more men."

"Everyone hold hands." He took his wife's hand and that of his son in his right hand and his daughter's and

Les's in his left. The others joined hands and they kneeled in a circle, heads bowed. Jim led them in prayer.

"Lord, we want to thank you for all the good things you have given each our families. We want to thank You for showing us the way to this valley and for the protection You have given us to this point in time. If it is in Your plans, help us through this day because we surely need Your help Lord. Forgive us of our sins in Your Holy name we pray. Amen.

He placed Les and Brad where he though they could be most effective and still be reasonably safe. He took a position next the wives and kids. It was almost time for him and his family to live-or die.

~~

Although they were not aware of it, the patrol finally made camp only three miles from where the Burgess family was holed up. The forced march last night had allowed them to make up several hours. They were breaking camp now after only four hours sleep. Tye had asked McClellan not to use his bugler any more and to keep all unnecessary noise down. He had one of those feelings he got every once in a while that something was fixing to happen. He just didn't know what.

162

An hour before the first gray of dawn was the darkest; Tye led them away from camp on foot, leading their horses. Tye had told the captain about his gut feeling and McClellan passed the word to his lieutenants to tell the men to carry their Sharps instead of leaving them in their saddle boot. McClellan had been around Tye on to many patrols when the scout had one of those feelings and it usually meant trouble.

~~

It was almost time Little Wolf thought as he looked over his shoulder at the graying sky behind him. During the last hour, while it was the darkest, several warriors had crept close to the ravine where the white men were hid. He had taken the leadership roll since he was the instigator in the ones with him leaving Yahzie and his visions. Only about one third of the band had gone with him and they were mostly the young ones like him. They would attack with the sun at their back making it hard for the white men to be accurate with their guns. Just a few minutes more he thought.

In the valley floor, the white men waited in the shallow arroyo. It was just beginning to be light enough to make out objects when Jim saw movement not forty yards in front of him. He whispered to Les and Brad.

"They've moved in close during the night. When I fire, start firing your Henry's in a sweeping motion, left to right. They are less than forty yards in front of us. Each of the women had a Colt and knew how to use it if they were about to be over run and knew to save one bullet.

Sweat poured off the men's faces even in the coolness of early dawn. Sweaty palms gripped their Henry's. Each man also had a Colt. They had extra ammunition for the Henrys within easy reach. Jim looked at the men. He figured they were as ready as they would ever be. He sighted in where he had seen the movement a moment earlier and took a deep breath and slowly exhaled. He squeezed the trigger and the crack of the Henry sounded like a cannon in the stillness of the morning.

An Apache yelped, stood and then collapsed and all hell broke loose. All three men were firing as fast as they could lever rounds in the chambers. Apache war cries split the air sending shudders up the men's and women's spines. The Apache screams along with the rifle fire was deafening. The three men were holding their positions and their fire was taking a toll, but Jim knew they were going to be overrun. The Apache had gotten to close to them during the night.

The patrol halted with the first shot. Tye jumped on Sandy as McClellan gave the order to mount. They moved out at a gallop down the valley toward the sound of the gunfire. That much fire could only mean one thing- Apaches.

When they could see what was happening, they halted. McClellan ordered his lieutenants to come to his side.

"Lieutenant Jefferson, you get A troop and Lieutenant Lewis, F troop up here. Sergeant Hill, you hold B troop here in reserve.

Hill, excited about the fight that was coming said. "But sir. I…"

Captain McClellan looked at him, eyes flashing anger. Mr. Hill, I gave you a damn order and you will follow it without question. Is that clear?"

"Yes sir."

He turned to Jefferson and Lewis. "Form a skirmish line on me and Tye- F troop to the left and A troop to the right. They started out at a gallop. McClellan turned to his bugler and shouted, "Sound charge, corporal and blow it loud." They increase their speed to an all out charge down the valley floor as the bugler cut loose.

The Apaches were almost in the ravine and Jim knew all was lost when everyone heard the bugle. The Apaches stopped their charge and were scrambling to get back up the canyon slope to their ponies. They quickly saw they were not going to make it and turned to fight the hated bluecoats.

Little Wolf and those who stayed with him on top of the rim were firing down on the soldiers who were in the midst of those warriors trying to get back to him and their ponies. He fired on an officer with shiny bars on his shoulders and grunted satisfaction when he saw him tumble off his horse. An Apache jumped on the officers mount only to be shot by a large man in a buckskin shirt. He fired at the big man, but missed.

Tye had shot the Apache on the horse and turned to fire at another on the ground. As he turned, he felt, or heard the whisper of a bullet as it passed by his head. He shot the Apache on the ground that had jerked a trooper off his mount and was about to club him when Tye's bullet struck him in the chest. Sandy knocked another down and trampled the screaming Apache with his hooves.

McClellan, who had emptied his revolver, was now swinging his saber at the swarming Apaches. He saw a trooper go down and being clubbed. He swung his saber and almost decapitated the hostile, but it was tool late for the trooper.

Tye shouted at McClellan to get his attention. When the captain looked his way, Tye pointed to the rim. McClellan saw the Apaches that were firing down on them. "Rally-rally," he shouted at the bugler who was staying close to him. The corporal put his bugle to his lips and blew the call to rally.

The few remaining Apaches on the ground were scrambling up the fairly steep slope. McClellan ordered a skirmish line and yelled for the men to follow him. Charging up the slope, the mounted troops quickly over run the few Apaches on foot trying to get away. The Apaches on the rim fired a volley of bullets and arrows at the advancing soldiers. One trooper took an arrow in the throat and fell from his mount only to be trampled by a horse coming up behind him. Two more took bullets and fell from their mounts. Private Garner fired his revolver at one the warriors on the rim and saw the hostile stumble and then fall forward, tumbling down the slope toward the fast advancing soldiers.

Private Carter, shot an Apache in the back that was scrambling up the slope and then fired a couple of shots at the one's on the rim. His bullets cut empty air and the heads disappeared under the rim. An Apache rose from the ground in front of him and struck his horses front legs with his war club. The horse and Carter went down hard. Carter, being an old cowboy and an excellent horseman, threw himself away from the horse. He rolled as he hit the ground knowing the Apache would be on him immediately. He was on his back looking at a grinning Apache that was in the process of swinging his club down on his head when the Apaches' eyes suddenly got real wide and something bloody was sticking out his chest. The warrior dropped the club, and stumbling a couple of steps, collapsed. McClellan reached down with his left hand and helped Carter to his feet. His right hand held the bloody saber.

"Thanks Captain. I thought I had checked it in." McClellan smiled.

"Find you a mount trooper." Carter found his pistol he had dropped when he hit the ground and shot his horse that had been crippled by the club. He found another horse and remounted.

When the troops scrambled over the crest of the hill they watched as the remaining Apaches rode off in the distance.

"Back down the slope men," McClellan ordered. "Make sure none of the hostiles are still alive." He turned to Lewis. "Lieutenant, get me a casualty report. He and Tye rode on down the slope to the people in the ravine.

The three men were helping their wives along with the two children climb out of the ravine when Tye and the officers arrived.

Jim turned to the officers and spoke. "God must have sent you captain. We were praying for a miracle and here you are." He shook the officers and Tye's hand vigorously. He introduced his wife, his wife's sisters and their husbands. He picked up his children and introduced them.

"Did God send you to help us?" the little girl asked Captain McClellan, her brown eyes big as saucers.

McClellan laughed for the first time in what seemed like years. He had taken his hat off when being introduced to the wives so he was not hindered by it when he leaned forward and kissed her on the cheek. "I didn't know it, but maybe he did. He does good things for people sometimes in a sneaky sort of way."

"Well, I don't know about everyone else in my family, but five minutes ago I figured we were all goners," Les, the youngest brother said shaking his head. "We were dead."

"What in the world are ya'll doing out here anyway?" Jim asked.

"Chasing the Apaches that attacked you." McClellan nodded toward Tye and added, "Tye's the best scout in the army and he was tracking the hostiles for us."

Jim shook Tye's hand. "An officer at Fort McKavett, Lieutenant Grimes I believe, said we might run into you if we got close to Fort Clark. He said you were the best scout he had ever seen. It's a pleasure to meet you and from all of us, please accept our gratitude." The two brothers shook Tye's hand as did the women. Tye was little red faced when the little girl in Jim's arms kissed him on the cheek.

Tye, always uncomfortable when the talk was about him, changed the direction of the conversation. "Are you folks figuring on settling here?"

Jim looked down the canyon. "It's a beautiful place. We figured we had found our home."

"It's beautiful okay, but did you wonder why no one had settled here?"

Jim nodded. "It crossed my mind."

"About a mile farther up the canyon is a spring that always holds water. It has been an important watering hole for the Apache for no telling how many years. They will not give it up. If you look around the floor of the canyon you will see three or four burned out homes of settlers who thought this valley was the perfect place also. We buried them here."

"You saying we should move on and find another place," Brad stated.

"I've never been one to tell anyone else what they should or shouldn't do," Tye replied. "But if I was you and had a family-yes, I would find another place."

Jim let out a sigh. "I think it best we move on." He turned to his wife and the rest of his family. "Let's get our things together and move on."

"I think that is wise Mr. Burgess. However, until this Apache problem is settled, it might be better for you and your family to go to Fort Clark. It's safe there plus I'm sure your wives and kids could use the rest. I will send a couple of my men with the dead and wounded back to Clark, and you can ride with them."

Jim looked at the women and saw in their eyes they agreed with the captain. "We'll take your kind offer captain." He reached out and shook McClellan's hand again. "We'll be ready in a minute." He left with his wife and family to gather their things."

McClellan turned to Tye. "They seem like good people, Tye."

"I've learned over the years, Captain, that for the most part, people who make a living off the land are the salt of the earth. They are honest and make no excuses for their successes or failures probably because the land does not compromise and the land will not be short changed. A man has to work it. Pour a lot of sweat and blood into it or it will not produce for him. It takes a special breed of men and women to make it out here. That's the reason I do what I do and that's the reason you are out here-to protect these special people."

McClellan smiled, "Damn Tye, that's the most words I ever heard come out of your mouth at one time in awhile." He chuckled again. "You're right though. They deserve a chance to make it and I'm going to do what I can for them as long as I can."

"Well, pick your men to take the dead and wounded along with the civilians to the fort so we can get after the Apaches." The troops watched in silence as the family moved out with the two soldiers, the four dead men and the severely wounded. As they disappeared over the hill, Tye led the troops on the trail of the Apaches.

Chapter Nineteen

The young warriors were not happy when they returned to camp where Yahzie and the others were. Many of the older warriors chastised them for being so foolish, their actions resulting in several dead and wounded. Yahzie did not say much. It was not too many winters ago he was young and hot-headed, looking for a fight to prove himself. He was glad the young ones were back even though they now had to gather their dead and bury them before continuing their fight against the invaders.

He sent his friend Little Bear ahead of them to make sure the soldiers were gone from the valley where the fight took place. He had asked the returning young men if they had seen a large white man in buckskins leading the bluecoats. More than one said they had seen him.

"Watkins," he said spitting out the name in disgust. *"If he is with them, then we must me twice as careful,"* he mused. As soon as that thought left his mind, another entered. *"Kill Watkins-kill the scout that thinks like an Apache and killing the rest will be so easy. Cut the head off the snake the body still moves for a short time even though it is dead. The soldiers will be like the body of the snake without Watkins, still alive-but dead."* He smiled. *"And besides, killing the scout would make me known as one of the great leaders among my people."*

He picked up his shield and with a mixture of roots, berries and clay to make paint, he painted the face of a bear on it. The bear had appeared in his dream. The bear stood on its hind legs and before him lay many soldiers, their dead eyes looking skyward. The great bear stood over the dead men and on his massive shoulders, Yahzie saw the faces of two other great Apache warriors, Tanza and Grey Owl. In the center of the massive beats chest, was the image of Yahzie's face. The warrior awoke from the dream sweating, his heart pounding. Yahzie took this dream, or vision, as meaning he had been given the strength of the bear to conquer his enemies and as long as he had his shield, he was invincible. He figured he was given the wisdom and cunning of the two greatest warriors he had ever known, Grey Owl and Tanza.

As he thought of this, he realized his goal in life had been laid out for him by the bear. Killing all the bluecoats and especially, the white scout who had killed Tanza and Grey Owl, the hated Watkins would be his greatest achievement. He knew he was going to be greater than any Mescalero Apache before him, maybe greater than the Chiricahua Apache he had heard about, Cochise.

~~

McClellan had lost four men in the encounter with the Apache. Six had been wounded and three of those had to be taken back to the fort. Lieutenant Jefferson was one of the wounded who had to be taken back leaving McClelland with one officer, First Sergeant Arnold, and two line sergeants. He knew most of the troops were veterans of many patrols, but he was still a little uneasy being an officer short. He knew even experience troops needed an officer to rally around when things got crazy. He had forty plus men and one officer and himself. "Thank God I have Tye and First Sergeant Arnold," he mumbled under his breath.

Tye, in front of McClellan and the column by several hundred yards, was on the trail of the hostiles. The trail was plain, the terrain fairly flat, so he was riding relaxed-at least more so than usual when on point. In the distance, thirty miles or so, he could see the blue shrouded mountains in Mexico which was the home of the Apache. Those mountains had been the homeland of the Apache for countless generations. *"Not much longer,"* Tye mused. *"The Mexicans are killing them for their scalps which the Mexican officials are paying bounties and we want their land."* He leaned forward and scratched Sandy on the neck and spoke softly in his ear.

"I feel for them, Sandy. They are a proud people, a hardy people who thrive in this land that can be so brutal to us." He reined Sandy to a halt and looked up at the position of the sun. "We'll wait here and see if the captain wants to give the men a break." A few minutes later the column caught up to them.

"What is it, Tye?" McClellan asked.

"Nothing Captain. We've been pushing pretty hard for the last few hours and I thought you might want to give the men and horses a break for a few minutes."

"Have we made up any time on the hostiles?"

Tye looked in the direction of the trail. "They are in no hurry. I'd say we have cut the time in half."

"Half!" McClellan bellowed out. "That means we are within two or so hours."

"Just about. Close enough we had better keep our eyes open."

McClelland turned to Lieutenant Lewis. "We are taking a thirty minute break. Pass the word to the men." McClellan and Tye dismounted and took care of their mounts. Afterwards, while they both sat on a large flat rock, Tye noticed McClellan cleaning his gun and smiled. Looking at the men lounging in the shade of the mesquites, he noticed them checking their weapons also. McClellan had taught the men well the lesson about taking care of their weapons that Tye had preached to him about on previous patrols.

Lieutenant Lewis, First Sergeant Arnold and the two line sergeants, Hill and Lambert walked up to them and sat down.

They talked among themselves for a couple minutes before Hill noticed Tye staring off toward the mountains, apparently lost in thought.

"Whatcha thinking about, Tye?"

Tye turned his head and looked at the men. "Apaches."

"About killing them?" Hill questioned.

"Killing them-hell no!" Tye blurted out.

McClellan knew Tye sometimes had spells where he was thinking of the Apache's way of life. He figured this was one of those times.

"Tell the good sergeants here what you are thinking, Tye." Tye looked at the captain who nodded his head.

Tye looked at Hill and then Lambert. "What do you two see when you look at the land?"

Hill laughed. "Nothing except mesquites, cactus and bushes."
Lambert nodded in agreement.

"That's the difference between you and the Apache."

"What do you mean?"

"The white man sees desolation and nothing else. The Apache sees a land full of food, medicine, and plants to make things he can use." The two men looked at each other with quizzical looks on their faces.

"Food!" Sergeant Hill said raising his eyebrows and laughed.

Tye continued. "Yes, food sergeant. If a man takes the thorns off the prickly pear's green pad and cooks it properly it is nutritious and the red fruit that grows on the pads is very sweet. Certain fruits, roots, and berries can be eaten while some leafy plants might be added to a rabbit stew. The sharp points of the yucca is used as needles. Other plants are used as medicine to treat sickness or wounds. For instance, the bark of the oak contains an agent which can be used to clean wounds and fight infection. The bark, sap, and leaves of the chaparral could be used for many purposes; treatment of stiff limbs, intestinal troubles, sore muscles, snake, scorpion, and spider bites and many more. They used certain plants and the fibers from tree bark for making rope and frames for their shelters. Tanned deer hides made fine, soft clothes and sinew from the skins for lashing things together. The Apache have thrived in this land where the white man would starve. Fifty or so years ago they were hunters and gatherers of food until the Mexican and the white man came wanting their land and killing them. They took their hunting skills and refined them to use in war and became great warriors, feared by everyone, even most other Indian tribes."

"Sounds like you like them, maybe want to be one of them murdering bastards," Hill said sarcastically. Arnold knew what was coming and cursed the sergeant under his breath.

Tye jumped to his feet, grabbed a handful of Hills tunic and jerked him up also, Hill's face only inches from Tye's face-a face darkened with anger. Hill's toes were barely touching the ground as Tye held the much shorter man up with one hand.

The line sergeant's eyes were as big as saucers and sweat broke out on his forehead as he looked in the scout's face-a face that was handsome a second ago but was now full of rage.

Tye spit out the words at Hill. "You are the exact reason that we are fighting this war with the Apache. You and others like you know nothing about them and don't want to know. Just kill them, that's all you know. The Calvary goes charging into a camp killing men, women, and children we call it a great victory. The Apache wipes out a wagon train and we call it a dastardly deed, a massacre, perpetrated by a bunch of murdering heathens'." He kicked Hills feet out from under him and dropped him on his butt on the hard ground. "I really don't know why I try to keep men like you from getting them selves killed." He walked quickly to Sandy, tightened his saddle girth and stepping into the saddle turned Sandy heading away from the startled men at a trot and quickly disappeared over the crest of a hill.

"Arnold looked at Hill who was still sitting on his butt. "You stupid bastard! Of all the idiotic things to say to that man who has been fighting Apaches since before you were born and has saved yours and every other mans ass in the patrol more than once from being killed. Hell, his father was killed by the Indians." He pitched Hill his campaign hat which had fallen from his head. "I wouldn't want to be in your shoes if you get in a position where you are fixing to get your ass killed and Tye was the only one around to help. There ain't a man here that wouldn't blame him if it just let your sorry ass die."

Hill swallowed the lump in his throat and slowly stood up. McClellan walked over to him. "All the men heard what you said Hill. I don't think they think a hell of a lot of you right now. When we get back, or should I say, if we get back I'll see to it your stripes are taken away." He turned to the men. "Private Garner."

"Yes Sir," the grizzled old veteran said stepping forward.

"You just got promoted to line sergeant."

"Yes sir," he answered and saluting. The men, who had grown to like the old veteran, were extremely happy. Many considered him a father figure.

McClellan spoke to First lieutenant Baker. "Get the men mounted and lets see if we can catch up to our scout.

"Yes sir." He turned to the men and ordered them to prepare to mount. A couple of seconds later he gave the order to mount and led the men away at a trot following behind McClellan. Lieutenant Lewis rode beside the captain and First Sergeant Arnold rode behind them with the trooper carrying the 'A' troop guidon flapping in the wind. Sergeant Lambert followed with 'B' troop and their guidon and newly appointed Sergeant Garner led 'F' troop. Sergeant Arnold had a feeling this patrol was headed for disaster.

Chapter Twenty

Zeb Cates sat in Jim's saloon at a back table sipping whiskey and trying to figure out what to do. He had been doing a lot of thinking about things since he was released from the guardhouse. He had made damn sure he had not gotten close to Tye's home and for sure, not close to his wife. He had never been whipped in a bare knuckle fight before and wasn't anxious to try the scout again. He had seen the guard in front of Tye's home and he felt certain they would not hesitate to shoot him if he so much as stepped toward Rebecca or the house.

He quickly downed the shot of whiskey, quickly filling it again from the bottle he had bought. He scratched his nose through the bandage that covered it. A broke nose, busted lips, and one eye that was still half closed were

184

reminders of the fight. If he had continued struggling after pulling his knife there was a not a doubt that Tye would have killed him. *'He should've killed me when he had the chance,'* he mused, *'because the next time I see him, I'll shoot first.'*

He downed another drink before realizing he was becoming light headed. He corked the bottle deciding he had had enough to drink for now. It had been a long time since he had gotten drunk and he sure as hell wasn't going to now and take a chance in getting himself in more trouble. He leaned back against the back wall and took stock of his situation.

'Yancey and Billy were stupid fools for coming out here. They had the whole damn country to raise hell in and they had to pick Texas- and why in hell here at Fort Clark. Also, why in hell did I feel obligated to avenge their stupid asses for getting themselves killed. So far I have managed to travel a thousand miles, get my butt kicked by a damn scout, and have the hospitality of the forts jail for a night. On top of that, not a person in this stinking town will even talk to me except the barkeep and that's just to ask me if I want another bottle. I guess he's my only friend-at least as long as I have money. He shook his head and in spite of things, he smiled. *'Watkins was right-no one knows me and*

no one I know back home would ever know what happened out here if I just went back. But, he mused, *I would know and I can't live with that. I come here to kill that scout and that's what I'm gonna do.* He stood up, grabbed his bottle and headed for the door. He had a room at the Sergeant Hotel. '*I'll go there, lock the door and get stinking drunk. At least I won't get into trouble there.*

Rebecca was lying in bed feeding the babies. Buff, at these times would go sit on the porch till the feeding time ended. He was happier than he had ever been in his life. Being a grandpa and living here with Tye and Rebecca had changed his life. Sure, he missed the excitement of being on scout and would always miss the old days of trapping beavers in the Rockies and the beautiful mountains, but this life here at Fort Clark with Tye and Rebecca was different. '*I never really realized what being part of a family meant. I didn't know what it meant to be loved and to love. Ever since I left my family all those years ago to go to the mountains I have been alone with just a few close friends. If I had died back then no one would have missed me, no one would really care.* A tear rolled down his weathered cheek. '*God knows I wished I had fell in love, had a home and children to raise and watch grow up instead of the life I led.* He stood up and shook his head. *'No, that's not true. I would never trade those years in the mountains. I would though wish I had done things different after those years. Maybe if I had settled down in one place I would have fallen in love and raised a family.* He looked at Los Moras Creek, the oaks and pecan trees lining the creek, and lastly, at a lonely hawk circling high above and mumbled out loud. *"I am going to make up for those years if I can. I'm going to enjoy my remaining time with people I love and I am going to spoil those two kids as much as I can."* He laughed so hard his shoulders shook.

~~

Tye was having a tough time. He missed Rebecca and sorely wished he was home holding his babies in his arms instead of leading a patrol. On top of that, what Hill had said reflected most soldiers' thoughts on the Apache. *'They made no attempt to understand the people they were fighting and had no intention to. The Apache on the other hand understood the white man completely. The white man would lie, steal, and kill to get what they wanted-the Apache homeland. The Apache knew the white man would not keep their promises to do things they wrote down on the papers (treaties) they signed-they never have. They were a race of people that wanted what the Apache had and would do anything to get it. It was simple and the Apache understood that. If the generals and higher ups had spent time living with the Apache as I had, known them up close, they were know they are an honorable people. Their word was like the white man's use to be-honorable and could be believed. The word lie is not even in their language. Taking the Apache's land is what this war is all about. This country is huge, plenty big enough for everyone, but co-existence will never happen. There is just too much hate and mistrust.'* He reined Sandy in. There was dust in distance but it was hard to tell if it was from riders or a dust devil. He watched for a minute and decided it was the latter. He nudged Sandy with his heels and continued his scout.

The patrol had ridden for several hours barely keeping their scout in sight. McClellan knew Tye was still upset or he would have stopped so the men could have a break. He studied the arid landscape through dust and sun glare redden eyes. It all looked the same. As many patrols that he had been on he still could become lost in this country at times. This, he figured, was one of those times. He did not have a clue where he was. He knew the Rio Grande was west, the direction they were traveling, but finding the fort again-he was not sure he could if something happened to Tye.

"Tye's stopped, Sir," Lieutenant Lewis said interrupting McClellan's thoughts. "He's coming back toward us."

McClellan raised his arm and the patrol came to a halt. He turned in the saddle and spoke to Sergeant Arnold. "Have the men dismount, sergeant. We'll take a short break." He turned back just as Tye rode up.

Tye saw the men dismounted and nodded. "Figured your men needed a break and to take care of their mounts, captain." He dismounted and taking his canteen he carried for Sandy, poured some water in his hat and let the horse suck it up.

"You okay?" McClellan asked looking at Tye.

"Yeah! I guess I sorter lost it earlier. Sorry about that."

"Hill was out of order with what he said."

"Maybe Captain, but I've got a feeling that is what most of the troops think whether they admit it or not."

"The only good Apache is a dead Apache," McClellan said. "I've heard high ranking officers; fellow officers, line sergeants, privates, and civilians say that."

"They just need to look at things from the Apache side. This land as far as they are concerned is theirs. They have occupied it for three or four generations. I, you, and any other man would fight to their last breath if they were in the Apaches place and invaders were taking your land and killing your women and children." Tye shrugged and added. "You've heard me argue that a dozen times. I'm tired of trying to change peoples mind. Between you and me captain, I'm thinking seriously about quitting this scouting business and try something else."

McClellan, who had been sitting on a rock next to Tye, stood up. "You can't do that, Tye. I and these men depend on you to keep us out of trouble."

Tye chuckled, "You can do fine without me captain. You are as good an officer as I have ever rode with. With men like Sergeant Arnold, Major Thurston, and others, things will be in good hands."

"You can't let something like Hill said make you make some rash decisions."

"It's not just what Hill said. I've had a letter from the governor for quite awhile offering me a position as a U.S. Marshall. Chasing bandits is dangerous, but nothing like tracking Apaches. The pay is better and I now have two children to support so it makes sense to me to at least consider it."

"Well, I personally hope you just consider it," McClellan chuckled. He looked at his men and then back at Tye. "How far are we behind the hostiles?"

"Three or four hours. They aren't in any hurry for some reason which bothers me some because they have to know we are chasing them." He looked at the position of the sun. "We've got about two hours of daylight left captain. Let's don't waste them." He mounted Sandy and trotted off.

"Mount Up!" McClellan shouted at the troops. A minute later, Lewis was beside McClellan as they headed out following Tye.

Up ahead, Tye sat on Sandy looking at three Apaches sitting on their ponies no more than a quarter mile away watching the scout. Tye studied the terrain to his left and then to his right to make sure no more were moving toward his position. He had a feeling this is where it was going to end-one way or another. He looked over his shoulder seeing McClellan and the patrol was almost to him. Looking back he saw the Apaches were gone. He looked around trying to find a good defensive position, but none were to be seen except for a small depression to his left about fifty yards.

"What's going on Tye?" McClellan asked as he rode up.

"Apaches. We had better fort up and get ready."

"Where?" McClellan asked looking around for some sort of protection presenting its self.

"Onliest place I see is that depression over there." the scout answered pointing with his Henry. He reined Sandy toward it. Arriving, he was surprised it was as big as it was. The walls were about two foot high at the lowest and a little over six at the most. It was thirty feet wide at the widest and maybe forty yards long. At one time it probably held water from a spring that had dried up a long time ago and was a buffalo wallow in recent years.

"We need two men captain that can find their way back to the fort," Tye said as they dismounted just outside the depression. In a few seconds two corporals, Lawrence and Crouch were with him and McClellan.

"Can you two find Fort Clark from here?" Tye asked. Both men nodded and acknowledged they thought they could. "Well, our lives are going to depend on you finding it." He picked up a stick and drew a rough map on the ground. "Go back the way we came for three miles and then turn south. You will hit the Old Mail Road. Go east and you will find the fort. Take my horse Sandy. Each of you will need three horses so you can switch out ever three miles or so. Gallop them, trot them and then gallop them. If they start faltering, walk them for fifteen or so minutes. Keep moving and you should be there by noon tomorrow. Get a patrol back here as soon as you can with extra horses and an ambulance. Take a canteen each for yourselves and a couple for the horses." He looked at McClellan. "They need to wait about fifteen minutes and then get out of here."

"You heard Tye. Get ready to leave and good luck." McClellan said shaking each mans hand. Within ten minutes. Apaches appeared on the hills to their right and left. "God Almighty! The captain exclaimed. "There must be a hundred of them."

"I don't think there's a hundred but there's more than enough to go around," Tye said. You had better set you defenses sir."

"Lieutenant Baker. You and Lieutenant Lewis set the men along the walls, evenly spaced. Put the horses in the end of this wallow where the walls are the highest and have two men with them. Have the men take one swallow from their canteens and then turn them over to Sergeant Arnold.

Sergeant, you are responsible for the water-give it out sparingly. Sergeant Garner, make sure the men check their weapons and have their extra ammunition from their saddle bags with them. Any questions?' The four men shook their heads. "Then let's get ready." Within less than two minutes, the men were spaced along the walls and their company guidon stuck in the ground behind them and flapping in the late evening breeze.

McClellan sat down beside Tye who was watching the hostiles on the hill in front of them. "Why did we not just make a run for it?"

"That's what the Apaches would want captain. They would love to catch us in the open or in a canyon. There are a thousand places between us and the fort or any other direction we go that is a good spot for an ambush. I'm always looking for a good spot to hole up in and for the last few miles; this is the only spot I have seen. I think we can hold them off here till help arrives.'

"But you just sent two men back the way we came. How are they going to get through?"

"I'm gambling that they had some men back there, but when they saw us dismounting to form a defensive position, they would leave to join the others on the hills."

"I hope you are right."

Tye nodded. "Me too sir."

McClellan looked over his shoulder and saw more Apaches on the hill behind them. He judged the distance and was thankful that the hostiles could not sit on the hill and shoot down on them. The more he looked around at the position the more he appreciated Tye's picking this spot. It seemed the scout always made the right decisions at times like this-he only hoped this one continued the trend.

As the men watched, the hostiles begin prancing their ponies back and forth and shouting what was probably insults at their hated enemy.

Corporals Lawrence and Crouch had their hands full almost as soon as they left. Less than a mile from the defensive position of the patrol, they had four Apaches chasing them. After a mile or so and after switching horses they were finally breathing a little easier as the Apaches were falling behind

Yahzie sat on his pony watching the scene before him. He was holding his warriors back which with their spoiling for a fight was hard to do. He knew the bluecoats were trapped and he had time to wait. He has watched as the two men left with the horses, but even if they got through his men he knew it would be at least two days before help arrived. There would be no soldiers left alive by that time.

He had sent Too-Shay to see if he could get more warriors to join them. There were several Apache haciendas within a few miles of where they were and his friend was very persuasive when he wanted to be. As he looked down the hill where the soldiers were he was amazed at how things looked the same as in his dream-his vision. He turned his pony around and walked him down the opposite side of the hill to where a small spring was surrounded by large oaks offering cooling shade. They would camp here for the night and decide the best way to attack the bluecoats.

Tye had taken in the terrain around him also. He did feel like it was defendable and maybe they had a chance to hold out until help arrives-if the two men got through.

"What are they waiting for?" McClellan asked.

"We're not going anywhere captain. They have all the time they need to do what they are going to do. There will be no moon tonight which will help them because they can get in close in the darkness and rush us at daylight."

"So you don't think they will attack until in the morning?"

"I don't think so, but like I've always said, you can never figure out an Apache. What I do know is that it is going to be a long night."

Chapter Twenty One

McClellan scanned the hill before him with his field glasses. Approximately thirty Apaches sat on their ponies spread across the crest. Looking west he could see Apaches, but they were moving and it was hard to get an accurate count. Turning around and looking at the hills to the north there were twenty or so sitting on the ponies watching. He was sure there a few east, the direction they had come from, just as Tye said.

The Apaches would have to charge through fairly open ground with little cover other than scattered low sage bushes and a few cedars. All of men were below ground so he felt better after digesting the situation. It was still serious because of the number of hostiles before him and he was sure that was not all of them. Also, his men had a limited

198

amount of water and they could expect no help until day after tomorrow. That is a long time to hold out against a well armed enemy who outnumbered you. He placed the glasses back in their case and resolved himself to doing what every soldier hated-waiting for hell to come his way.

On the other side of the hill Yahzie sat beside the small spring with Little Bear and two older warriors. He was anxious to kill the bluecoats, but smart enough to ask advice from the older, more experienced warriors sitting beside him.

"My father taught me to always listen to the older, more experienced warriors before making a decision. Please give me your thoughts on the best way to attack the soldiers."

Chuntz, the older of the two was well known among his people as a fearless warrior who in his younger years killed many Comanche warriors and took many captives. He was known not to be reckless in his actions and had given council to other Apache leaders.

"The bluecoats are trapped but are in a good position. There is no need to go rushing down the hill to over run them and having many warriors killed. My council would be to be patient. They have limited water and food and in the canyon, it will be hot. We can keep them awake during the night and tomorrow by having our best shooters fire at them occasionally and beating our drums. When the sun comes up on the second day we could attack as the sun comes over the hill. With it at our back the soldiers will have a hard time finding us in their sights."

Yahzie nodded. "It is wise council Chuntz gives. We will do as he suggest."

"The young ones will be hard to hold back till then," Little Bear said.

"It will be up to us to convince them otherwise," Contanza, the other older warrior suggested.

Yahzie spoke. "It will be dark soon. We will assemble our warriors here, around this spring and tell them what we will do and why we are doing it. Too-Shay should be here by morning with more of our brothers." He stood up. "Go and bring our brothers here, but leave a few scattered along the tops of the hills to keep the bluecoats from slipping away. Explain our plan to those who stay." Little Bear and the two older warriors left.

"What are they up to?" McClellan asked Tye as he watched a lot of hostiles on the move.

"About what I expected," Tye answered. "They are gathering their men together for the night. They will leave just enough warriors scattered along the crest of the hills to watch for us trying to sneak out during the night while the rest spend their time dancing, beating their drums and working them selves into a killing frenzy."

"I figured they were already ready for that."

Tye chuckled. "Your right, but their hollering and beating their drums will keep most of us awake all night and then they will probably hit us at first light hoping to catch us napping."

A grunt from behind them was followed by the heavy report of a rifle. Turning, both men saw a soldier holding his shoulder, blood pouring out a large hole high in his back.

"What the hell?" McClellan exclaimed as he looked in the direction the shot had come from.

"They have a 'big fifty' somewhere on that hill," Tye said as he crawled to the wounded man.

McClellan shouted to the men. "They have a Sharps fifty caliber so keep your heads down." A rock exploded and showered two soldiers with cutting rock fragments followed by the familiar boom of a big fifty.

"Damn," one of the men cursed as he wiped blood from a cut on his cheek from the rock splinters.

"Stay down" McClellan shouted again. "Keep your damn heads down." He looked over to where Tye was bent over the wounded man. "How bad?"

"He's hit pretty hard, captain, but it went clean through which is good. If we can get the bleeding stopped he'll be down awhile but will be okay." Tye answered holding pressure on a torn undershirt over the exit wound on the man's back. Tye looked at the wide eyed private kneeling next to him staring at the blood soaked shirt. "Put your hands on the shirt and press down and don't let up." The private placed shaking hand over the wound and pressed down. "Just hold the pressure private."

He crawled back over to where McClellan sat his back against the dirt wall. "We're in trouble with that gun out there."

McClellan nodded in agreement. "There ain't much we can do about it."

"Maybe after dark, I can find it," Tye said.

"You're going out there-by yourself," McClellan said, not believing what he just heard.

"By myself," Tye answered. "I can get around just about as good as an Apache. Maybe I can find it and eliminate it."

"I don't know Tye. Sounds like suicide to me."

"I know it sounds crazy, but if we don't get it, tomorrow could be a hell of a long day with a lot of casualties. I need to leave about midnight when things are quiet."

"I still think its crazy, but I see your point about tomorrow. I'll pass the word to the men when you leave and what you are doing so they won't get trigger happy."

Tye nodded and leaned back against the wall and pulled his hat down over his face to try and get a little sleep before leaving. McClellan looked at him and then at the other men in the depression. He saw a lot of tension and fear in the faces and then he saw First Sergeant Arnold and newly appointed line sergeant, Garner. Both men were speaking with the men around them, reminding them they were soldiers and to act like one. He could hear Garner's words to a very nervous private that looked like he was sixteen, but was probably twenty or so.

The private stared at Garner, but was not hearing what the sergeant was saying, simply stared with eyes as big as saucers. McClellan recoiled a little when he heard the slap as Garners palm struck the privates cheek. "Now listen to me and pay damn attention to what I am saying- you hear?" The private rubbed his cheek and nodded his head. McClellan could tell the slap had a positive effect on the private as well as some of the men around him.

Garner looked around at the men surrounding him. "We're in a tight, I won't lie to you about that. If you want to survive this you had better do a few things such as; one- accept the fact you are no different than anyone else- we are all scared, but you have to handle it like the man you are; two-follow orders without hesitation; three-keep your cool when the Apache come screaming down that hill; and lastly, when you shoot make sure you hit what you are aiming at. He spoke loud enough for all the men to hear. He looked at the far end of the depression where Private Caxton huddled against the wall. "Starting with you Caxton, I want each man to sound off. Caxton you are one, and Holt," who was next to Caxton, "you are two. Now sound off." Caxton hollered one, Holt bellowed two, and so it went around the depression until each man had sounded off his number. "Now listen up, Garner ordered. "Odd numbers will fire first and then the even and then odd and then even. This way, fire will be steady instead of everyone firing at once and then everyone having to reload at once.

Understood?" Around of aye's and yes sirs followed. Tye raised his hat up and looked at McClellan and smiled.

"He'll do, Captain."

All was quiet when Tye stood up and stretched. It was almost midnight and pitch dark. The scout took off his hat, his belt and holster, and his leather shirt. He did not want anything on him that could make a scratching sound on the sage and mesquite or rocky ground. He took five extra shells for his Colt from his belt and put them in his pants pocket. He would carry his Colt in his left hand and his Bowie in his right and nothing else.

McClellan ordered the men to move in a little closer so they could hear him. He spoke in a low voice, just loud enough that everyone could hear him.

"Listen up. All of you know what's probably going to happen tomorrow. We can hold off a charge or two, but they will keep us ducking all day with that damn buffalo gun. The best thing we can do is try to eliminate it. Tye will be slipping away in a minute to try and find the Apache with it and do just that. I'm telling you this because I don't want him shot by one of you thinking he is an Apache when he comes back. Now get back to your positions and get some rest. You with the even numbers watch for two hours and then switch with the odd numbers watching. Good luck."

The men hurried back to their post each thanking God it was Tye and not them going out to find the hostile with the big gun. Private Jolson, the man who was hit by the shell from the fifty earlier was resting comfortable-at least as comfortable as a man could that had been shot and had nothing for the pain whispered to Tye 'good luck'. Tye patted him on the shoulder, gave him a smile, and climbed out of the depression headed into what he knew, could be a lot of trouble.

Chapter Twenty Two

Tye could only see a few feet at best so he made his way toward the base of the hill slowly and carefully, placing his moccasin foot down carefully to avoid breaking twigs and making undue noise. Experienced in this type of warfare he made no more noise than a lizard scurrying over rocks. Knowing a mistake could cost him his life made a man in a situation like this very careful. He stopped every minute to listen. He would be perfectly still, barely breathing for a minute before moving on.

He had been gone from the 'wallow' for twenty minutes and was more than half way up the slope when he heard a slight noise. He dropped from his crouched position he had been in to kneeling behind a thick sage. Holding his breath, he heard it again. It was the sand of cloth scathing on brush. All of a sudden an Apache was beside him, three feet a way staring down the slope unaware of Tye. When the warrior moved a step farther down the slope and had he back to Tye, the scout swung the three pound Colt and the barrel caught the brave in the back of the skull. The only sound was the limp body hitting the ground.

Tye took a deep breath and exhaled slowly, trying to relax. *"That was close,"* he mused. *"Ole boy, you had better be damn careful.* He moved up the slope but stopped every two or three steps to get his bearings and to listen.

Thirty minutes later he had reached the crest without seeing any more Apaches. He moved to his left which, if his calculations were right, was where the shots from the Sharps came from. Moving silently he was startled to find himself three feet from an Apache who was standing with his back to Tye relieving his bladder. Just as he finished, Tye placed his hand over the man's mouth, jerked his head back and drove his Bowie into the man's chest. The Apache stiffened and struggled for a couple seconds and then went limp in Tye's arms. He lowered the dead man quietly to the ground. Moving a few feet farther he was surprised to find the gun he was looking for leaning against a large boulder. Picking the gun up he moved back to the dead Apache and took a handful of cartridges he found in a deer skin pouch and stuffed them in his pocket He had taken only a few steps down the hill when he heard a shout below him and to his left. They had discovered the warrior he had knocked out. All the Apaches were alert now and moving, searching for the white man. Another shout went up behind him as they found the dead Apache who had been shooting the buffalo gun. They were coming in a hurry down the slope toward him.

"No sense trying to hide now," he mumbled out loud. He stuck the Bowie in the sheath in the top of his right boot and switched the Sharps to his left hand and had the Colt cocked and in his right. He took off down the slope not worrying about noise now. A warrior rose up in front of him and Tye blasted him square in the chest with his colt, the slug knocking the man backwards down the slope. Bullets were hitting rocks and cutting limbs from the sage and cedars all around him as he ran and stumbled down the slope.

"DON'T FIRE UNLESS YOU KNOW IT'S NOT TYE," MClellan shouted to his men hearing and seeing the flashes of ten or so guns on the slope. A few seconds later they heard Tye shouting.

"I'M COMING IN!" Ten seconds later a exhausted Tye stumbled into the depression into waiting arms of a couple troopers. McClellan was elated at not only that Tye was safe, but he saw the buffalo gun was in his hand. Tye sat on his but, head down and breathing hard.

A private, looking at Tye hollered, "Your hit Tye." Other troopers around Tye then saw the blood running down the scouts left arm.

"I'll look at it in a minute. Let me catch my breath."

"I'll look," McClellan said scooting over to where Tye sat. "You've been hit high on the shoulder Tye."

Tye raised his arm and looked. "Bullet just creased me some captain. Not bad enough to worry none about."

"Let me make that decision." McClellan said. He looked at the closest trooper to him. "Get to my horse private and look in the left saddle bad and bring me the shirt that is in it."

"Yes sir."

He took a canteen from Sergeant Arnold and poured a small amount on the wound to wash the dirt out and handed it back to the sergeant. The private came back with the shirt and McClellan ripped a sleeve off and wrapped Tye's upper arm tight with it and tied it off. "It's just about stopped bleeding and maybe that wrap will keep some of the dirt out."

"It's fine Captain-thanks. In all the running and shooting I didn't realize I'd been hit."

"What happened out there?" McClellan asked. Several troopers were straining to hear Tye's reply.

I met one Apache coming down the slope as I was going up and dispatched him with the barrel of my Colt across his skull. Once I reached the top I stared working my way toward where I figured the Apache was with the 'fifty'." He chuckled a little. "I found him with his back to me taking a leak. I let him finish and then took him out with my Bowie."

"Letting him finish was mighty thoughtful of you Tye," a voice from the darkness said. Everyone had a nervous laugh at the remark.

Tye continued with his report. "I found the gun and just as I picked it up I heard a commotion. I knew the first Apache I had hit with my Colt had been discovered so I took off down the slope. One came out of the darkness in front of me and I shot him with my Colt. It was crazy after that. I was running and stumbling down the slope. My stumbling must have made me a hard target to hit because some the shots came from close range." He laughed and added, "I'm sure the Apaches were surprised there was a crazy white man among them."

"I don't give a damn what they thought," Private Jolson said. "You got the one who shot me and got the gun."

"Amen," came from several throats at once.

"Get back to your positions men," McClellan ordered. He sat down beside Tye. "Did you see anything out there I should know about?"

"A lot of Apaches," Tye chuckled, and then added in a serious tone. "There were several Apaches below and beside me as I made my way down the slope. I think they are moving as close as possible to us in the dark preparing for a rush from the east as the sun come sup."

"Do I need to put all my men on this side then?"

"I would take half of them and leave the other half over there just in case. I could be wrong and they could come from both sides."

"I've been around you enough to know how your intuitions are. I'll move half of them over here." He crawled along the bottom of the depression to where Sergeant Arnold kneeled and spoke in a low voice. "Sergeant."

"Yes sir."

"Tye thinks they will come from the east with the sun behind them at first light. He also said they were moving in close in the dark so they will be on us quick." Arnold nodded his understanding of the situation.

"What do you suggest sir?"

"Take half the men on your side and put them on the side facing east. Have them be aware the hostiles could only be yards away when the come. Make sure they alternate their firing so while one is firing the man beside him is reloading. Make sure they have their sidearm's handy and if need be use them instead of their carbines. Understood?"

"Yes sir. I'll take care of it sir." McClellan moved back to his spot by Tye.

Two hours before first light the sound of a lot of horses brought the Apache camp alive. A brave rode in announcing that Too-Shay was arriving with many warriors. Yahzie rose from his blanket at the first sound of the horses. He was the first to greet Too-Shay.

As he looked at the braves pouring into camp he was amazed. "How-how did you get so many?" he asked as his friend jumped from his mount and clasped Yahzie's shoulder with his hand.

"The word was already in the camps of the Apaches about Yahzie. The young men were ready to come to you."

Yahzie looked again at the young warriors as they continued to come into camp. "How many?"

"Five times the number of fingers on both hands."

Yahzie sat back down on his blanket and Too-Shay sat beside him. The amount of warriors in the camp had doubled in a couple minutes and the feat that his friend had accomplished overwhelmed him. He now had almost a hundred warriors that were anxious as he was to kill the white-eyes, to run these people out of their land.

He turned to Too-Shay and Chuntz. "Gather our brothers around so we may talk." In a few minutes, he was surrounded by all the warriors that was not on the hills watching the soldiers. He looked all around him, studying their faces before he spoke. He was that many of them were very young and could not be experienced.

"I am Yahzie," and before he could say another word, loud shrieks poured from almost a hundred throats and his name could be heard being called repeatedly. He raised his arms and silence fell on the camp as all gave full attention to what their anointed leader was going to say.

"My heart is bursting with joy that so many of my brothers have joined me in my fight to rid our land of all invaders. Those of you who know me know I have killed many Comanche and Mexicans in battle. You also know white men came into my camp and killed my family. What started as a quest for vengeance against the men who did that deed has turned into a hate for all whites. To have a land, our land that we can go and come as we please is my dream as it should be yours. You should be able to take a woman as your own and to have sons that you can teach the ways of our fathers and to live the life of an Apache warrior. I want to be left alone in my land, Apache land. We can start fulfilling our dream now by killing the bluecoats we have trapped in the canyon over the hill and then all the whites that are moving into the land given to us by Ussen, the creator."

The warriors jumped to their feet, raising their rifles over their heads and screaming their leaders name and working themselves into a killing frenzy that always put fear into the Apache's enemies.

The noise coming from over the hill had the soldier's attention.

"What the hell is going on all of a sudden with all that screaming?" McClellan asked Tye. This was the same question that was on every troopers mind also.

"I think we had better get ready Captain. They are working themselves into a mood that we ain't going to like and all hell is going to break loose in an hour or so." As the last word passed his lips, a drum starting beating, the shrieks increased, and shots were fired.

McClellan started to give the order for the men to get ready, but a quick look at the faces of the troopers close by told him the order wasn't necessary. They were in position, they were alert, and he knew they were like him-scared to death. They were waiting for a soldier's worse nightmare-facing a charge by screaming Apaches that wanted to not only kill you, but butcher you so bad your mother would not recognize you.

Tye rolled and lit a cigarette. McClellan wondered how in the world he could do it without spilling any tobacco. His own hand was shaking so bad he could not have even got the makings out of his pocket without dropping them.

Tye had his repeating Henry and the rest had their single shot carbines. He had moved the injured Jolson to his side. Not only to protect him, but he had given the private a box of cartridges so he could reload the Henry for him while he used his Colt. He looked at the sky which had the first streaks of gray beginning to appear.

"*Won't be long now,* he mused. He checked his Henry and his Colt for the umpteenth time. He reached down and pulled his Bowie from its sheath and stuck it in the ground beside him. He looked at the top of the hill when the trooper on his left mumbled.

"Sweet Mother of God!"

"What the," Tye said out loud. Through the dimness of early morning, close to a hundred Apaches sat on their ponies on top of the hill about four hundred yards away.

McClellan nudged Tye in the side. "Where did they all come from?"

"I don't know Captain, but this is going to get real nasty in a few minutes."

McClellan turned and spoke loud enough for all to in the wallow to hear.

"Stay calm men. Hold your positions and don't fire until I give the command to fire. Make your shots count. Fire once with your carbines and then use your pistols. Understood?"

A loud chorus of 'yes sirs' came back to him and each man turned back to watch the hill. They waited for hell they were sure was come their way.

McClellan whispered to Tye. "Say something to the men Tye. They would feel better about things if you would. You know what they think of you."

Tye thought about it for a moment and then begin speaking in a steady voice loud enough for all to hear.

"I know you are nervous and scared. We all are."

"You ain't scared Tye," a young private that looked like a teenager said.

"Yes I am private. Only a crazy man wouldn't be at times like this. If you want to live, listen to what I say. First of all, admit you are no different than anyone else when it comes to being scared. Accept the fact that when a man goes into battle being scared is normal and a man who says he isn't is crazy. Channel your fears into wanting to do your best not to let the man down that is next to you. You knew when you enlisted that was going to happen sooner or later, so handle it like a man. When they come, take a deep breath and then exhale slowly. This will calm you some. Take aim and don't miss. Take care and fight like hell and we'll get through this. Hold your fire until the captain tells you to fire. Remember, if you panic, you are dead and so will your buddy that was depending on you to watch his back. Don't let him down."

Tye turned back to McClellan and in almost a whisper said, "We're in for a whipping if the men don't hold. I know most of the men and been through things like this with them and they will be okay. It's the ones I haven't seen before that bothers me. If just a couple or three of them panic, we're done. I figure we have about one hour and then they'll be coming down that hill."

"I'll see if maybe we can prevent that from happening," McClellan whispered back. He turned and in a tone loud enough to carry the length of the wallow said, "Sergeant Arnold."

"Yes Sir." Arnold replied from his position.

"Make your way to me."

"Will do," Arnold replied while making his way past the men toward the captain. He slid in beside McClellan. "Yes Sir?"

In a voice just loud enough for Arnold and Tye to hear he told his First Sergeant that he wanted an experience man beside every man that he knew had not been in combat before and that they are to make damn sure the recruits do what they are supposed to do. Arnold nodded and left to carry out the order.

Adam Carter was no different than every other man in the wallow-he was scared to death waiting for hell that was shortly coming his way. He was second guessing the decision he had made a few months ago as to his joining the army or going to prison. Busting rocks all day didn't seem so bad right now. He looked around at the men near him. All of them were mumbling to themselves. '*praying for forgiveness and protection,* he mused. He looked at the sky that was turning gray with approaching dawn and lowered his head.

"Lord I haven't spoken to you since I asked you to help me stay out of prison. I'm truly sorry about that." He turned his face up toward heaven. *"I'm not asking you to spare me Lord, but I am asking that you give me the strength and courage to help my brothers here. Don't let me let them down. If it's not in your plan for me to live through this day please be with my family, my ma and pa and my little brother Jason. Protect them and let them live their lives out in good health. I know you are listening Lord, just as you have in the past and I thank you for that. Amen."* He felt better and knew he could now accept his destiny whatever it was.

Sergeant Arnold had repositioned his men putting veterans on both sides of the eight men he knew had no battle experience and then took up his position. He was nervous and scared, but it was no different than the other ten or eleven times he had encountered Apaches. A sudden thought brought a smile to his lips. He remembered a time similar to this when he was with Tye. The scout had come up with a plan and when he asked Tye if it would work Tye answered "Well if it don't then it's like the Apaches say, it's a good day to die. He thought that was a pretty damn stupid remark at the time, but reflecting back, it was true. A man does what he can and if things work out, great and if they don't…well. He looked back up the hill and waited.

The newly appointed Sergeant Garner was also watching the hill, his cheek resting on the stock of his Sharps. His experience in Indian warfare was mostly with the Comanche's. He had limited experience with the Apache, but he had listened intently to conversations in the quarters at the fort and around camp fires when on patrol. He figured the Apache were meaner than the Comanche and that scared him some. He knew he would handle himself well. Hc had several vicious fights with the Comanche and as a lawman had faced down several outlaws. He intended to make sure every man around him held their ground and did what they were paid their thirteen dollars a month and two meals a day to do. He looked up again at the hill and waited.

Yahzie sat on his pony beside his friend Too-Shay and Little Bear.He was furious when he saw that clouds would block the suns rays that would have been in the bluecoats' eyes. He figured they expected him at first light so he decided to attack early, hoping to catch them a little off guard.

As he waited for it to get light enough that the horses could run without stumbling in the darkness his mind went back a few years. He was the son of Yellow Wolf, the greatest warrior in his camp. He himself was now a great warrior because of the things his father had taught him. His mind went forward to the recent killing of his family by six white men. He sorely missed holding his woman during the long nights, but he missed his son more. He was approaching the age the Yahzie could begin teaching him the things his father taught him; reading sign, tracking, fighting with knives, tomahawks and guns,; the ways of the Apache warrior; but most of all respect for his elders. He would teach him how important honor was and to never lie. All those dreams were gone now, taken from him by the white man just like they take ever thing else they want. They will lie, steal and kill to get these things.

"It is time," he said out loud and turned his pony to face the warriors. He raised his Henry above his head and pumping his arm up and down began shouting "It's a good day to die!" The other braves took up the shrieking and soon it was chaos. Yahzie turned back and taking a lance held it up above his head and every brave quit his shrieking and watched. Yahzie pointed the lance toward the soldiers and then dropped the point toward the wallow at the bottom of the hill and at the same time kicked his pony toward the soldiers and with a hundred shrieking warrior's right behind him had his in full flight down the slope.

Chapter Twenty Three

"HOLD YOUR FIRE," McClellan shouted above the noise. The ground shook from the pounding of four hundred hooves. Add the shouts of a hundred Apache warriors and it made a frightening scene for even the most experienced soldiers. On they came and every soldier wondered what the hell the captain was waiting for as bullets and arrows whizzed by or struck the dirt in front of them. Still McClellan waited until even Tye wondered what was happening, but just as the question entered his mind, McClellan hollered, "FIRE"

The boom from twenty five sharps firing their .52 caliber slugs and the sharp crack of Tye's Henry repeater added to the noise. A few warriors were knocked off their ponies, but more horses were hit than Indians. The warriors whose horses were hit were quickly on their feet and charging down the hill. Tye, firing as fast as he could work the lever on the Henry was taking a heavy toll on both horses and Apaches.

Apache arrows and bullets were taking their toll among the soldiers. A private by the name of Jones that was next to Carter was hit in the throat by a arrow. He clawed at the dirt with his hand in agony, choking on his own blood for a full minute never taking his eyes off Adam as if he was expecting him to help him. Adam glanced at him a couple times but he was busy trying to stay alive as the Apaches were less than thirty yards away and threatening to overrun the troopers.

Smoke from the rifles, hand guns, and the thick, choking dust raised by the ponies' hooves made it hard to tell enemy from friend. A man had to shoot at or swing his blade at anything that moved at times. Sergeant Garner was on his back in the wallow with an Apache on top of him that had hit him like a battering ram when he flung his body from his pony. Garner had held on to his carbine and this action saved him. He had the gun by the stock in his right hand and the barrel in his left and held in front of his face as the war club the Apache had was coming down intending to crush his skull. The steel of the barrel stopped the downward arc of the club much to the surprise of the Apache. The warrior was even more surprised as Garner released the barrel he held in his left hand and swung the gun with his right like a club catching the Apache on the right side of his head. Stunned, the brave fell to the side and Garner smashed his skull with the butt of his Sharps.

McClellan was on his back with an Apache on top of him who had his Bowie stuck to the hilt thru the captain's right shoulder. Tye swung his Henry and caught the warrior in the back of the head. He fell unconscious on top of McClellan who pushed him off of his chest with his left hand. He raised himself up and picked his Colt up with his left hand and prepared to defend himself again.

The Apaches, for the most part and Tye was thankful, were staying on their ponies and riding back and forth about twenty to thirty yards in front of the wallow firing at the bluecoats from horse back. A direct assault would have been disastrous for the soldiers. Firing from a running horse was not contusive to accuracy nor for the soldiers firing at men on horseback thru smoke and dust. There was a lot of shooting from both sides and as in most battles only a small percentage of bullets and arrows were finding a live target, but when you have that many bullets coming into a confined area, some did.

The fight had lasted for about four minutes and then it was over. The Apaches were gone and the men in the wallow, the ones still alive at least, took a deep breath and looked around as the smoke and dust were blown away by the light breeze. Even the battle harden veterans were shocked at the scene.

There was at least seven dead or wounded Apaches inside the wallow with them. They were all dead damn quick as well as were three or four wounded that were outside the wallow. Dead and wounded soldiers were every where.

McClellan, who was sitting up with his wound being attended to by Tye, shouted for Lieutenant Lewis.

"He's dead sir," a voice farther down the wallow echoed back. "Shot right between the eyes sir."

"Damn," McClellan cursed and then shouted, "Sergeant Arnold."

"Sir?" came a voice from some where in the smoke and dust from farther down the wallow.

"Get me a casualty report and the status of our ammo and water."

"Yes sir."

McClellan grimaced as Tye removed his shirt to look at the shoulder wound. "That's a nasty wound, Captain," he mumbled.

"Hell man, don't you think I know that-hurts like hell."

"Be right back," Tye said. He scrambled down the wallow stepping over dead Indians and soldiers, his eyes taking in the ghastly scene as he moved. Blood was everywhere and as he moved he noticed there weren't too many soldiers who weren't injured, some just scratches and others horribly injured. When he got to where the horses were he found Sandy and after reaching in his saddle bags and pulling out a clean shirt, headed back to McClellan.

Arnold arrived at the captain the same time as Tye.

"Eight dead, Sir, and thirteen wounded. All the wounded can still fight except three. Our ammo is good, but we are going to be short of water before the day is out-if we live that long."

"How many hostiles?"

'Not sure," Arnold replied. "Apaches have a way of carrying off their dead, but I counted twenty-two outside the wallow and seven inside."

"Thank you Sergeant. Go take care of your men and give the severely wounded some water. The others give one good drink and keep what is left of the water under your guard."

"Yes Sir."

"We hurt them pretty good, Captain. Almost thirty dead and certainly a lot wounded," Tye said ripping the clean shirt to make bandages. "I don't think they will hit us again today," he said wrapping the shoulder and making a sling. He looked up at the sky and the clouds moving in. "Cold weather may be moving in."

"Cold?" McClellan questioned looking up at the sky.

"Texas weather, sir. This is December and it can change quickly."

"Why do you figure they quit? They pretty well had us."

"Like I've said a hundred times captain," Tye answered, "You can never be sure what an Apache is going to do. I figure they will watch us the rest of the day to make sure we don't try to escape the trap and spend some time making new medicine."

"New medicine?"

"Apaches are like most Indian tribes in that they are very superstitious. For instance they believe in good medicine and bad medicine as far as war is concerned. If they win, their medicine was good, but if things don't go as planned, its bad medicine and needs to be changed."

"How do they change it?" a grimacing McClellan asked as a new wave of pain shot through his shoulder.

That question is why Tye thought so much of the captain. He was always trying to understand the Apache, not just trying to hunt them down and kill them.

"Sometimes when they feel their medicine is bad they will just leave to fight another day. Other times, they will elect a new leader since the one they had had bad medicine. I've known times that if their leader is well enough thought of as a warrior they will give his medicine another chance."

"What are they going to do now? We hit them pretty hard."

"We're not going to get off easy, sir. I'm betting this Yahzie is a damn well thought of warrior and because of that, he's going to get another shot at us."

"Another attack like we just faced?"

"I think he's to smart for that. He'll come at first light from at least two directions."

"You pretty sure about that?"

"About as sure as one can ever be about what an Apache is going to do."

"Sergeant Arnold!"

"Yes sir," the sergeant replied as he kneeled beside the captain.

"Tye here doesn't think the Apaches will hit us again today so I want you to have ever third man on watch and the rest resting. Switch every two hours. Have at least two men watching the hill behind us. Understood?'

"Will do sir."

"Sergeant."

Arnold turned back toward McClellan. "Sir?"

"Give the wounded a little extra water in a few minutes."

Arnold gave the captain a big smile. "Will do sir." He turned to leave, but turned back to the captain. "How's the shoulder?"

"Hurts like hell."

"At least you are alive and alert, sir. The men and me are thankful for that," he said before turning around and moving back down the wallow to check on the wounded and set the schedule for watching and sleeping. McClellan smiled despite the pain in his shoulder.

It hadn't been long ago, he mused, *that the men would not care one way or another whether I was alive or dead-probably most wished I was dead.* He had been an arrogant officer who did things strictly by the book with no deviations. He would not listen to anything the scouts, including Tye, said nor the men who had been here a long time and had seen just about everything the Apache could throw at a troop. He knew it all as far as what the Point had taught him, but he didn't know squat about fighting Apaches. The men despised him and would do anything to get out of going on patrol with him. That all changed one day when his arrogance almost got himself and several of his men killed. Tye saved his life and his career that day. The scout had talked to him pretty sternly that day and set him straight on what it took to be a good officer and what it took to have the men trust him and his decisions. That humbling event had changed him as a man and as an officer. The men no longer tried to get out of going on patrol with him and he had the one thing he always craved- respect. He could say without a doubt it was because of Tye.

His thoughts were interrupted by Tye's voice. "I noticed Private Downy was injured and Private Caxton was hovering over him like a mother hen."

"What's unusual about that?"

"Well sir, I heard they had quite a dislike for each other."

McClellan attempted to laugh, but it hurt too much. "Caxton was a Rebel and Downy was a Yank in the war. They both fought at Chickamauga where there were 34,000 casualties. The Rebs had the yanks on the run that day and Caxton would not let Downy forget it. They argued only when they were drinking. The rest of the time they were pretty close buddies."

McClellan was tired so he lay back down and tried to forget the pain, but it wasn't working. He looked at the men who except for those on watch were settling in for a long day. God knows his would be.

Chapter Twenty Four

Zeb Cates wasn't a patient man. He was getting tired of sitting around waiting for Watkins to get back off patrol. He had stayed in his hotel room except to eat. His nose hurt like hell, and his face was so swollen he didn't even recognize himself in the mirror. He was sure of only one thing; he would not try whipping that sonofabitch again with his fist or with a knife. He believed all the stories he had heard about the scout were true and he would probably be hard pressed to kill him even with a gun.

He also knew the smart thing to do would be to go back home and forget this vengeance idea. He smiled as a thought crossed his mind. *I've been accused of a lot of things but being smart was never one of them. I've got to plan this out and not do anything without thinking it out first. Like he said, the Apaches and bandits have been trying to kill him for years.* He sat on the bed and pulled on his boots. "What I need right now is a damn drink." He stood up, opened his door and headed down the stairs hurrying to the nearest saloon.

He walked into Jims and after looking inside, walked to the bar where he was greeted by Jim-and a double barreled shotgun that was pointed at his belly.

"What's this?" Zeb asked.

"I'm particular about who I serve in my saloon hombre and I don't want to serve you-now get. There's another saloon just down the street that I'm sure you will be welcome."

Zeb put out hands, palms up. "Why won't you serve me a damn drink?"

"Two reasons; one being your related to those sorry pieces of shit Cates brothers, and two, you're wanting to kill a friend of mine. For two cents, I'd cut you in half with this here scatter gun and save Tye the trouble of killing you."

"You seem pretty sure he's going to kill me," Zeb said smiling.

"You are a walking dead man Cates. Hell, five hundred Apaches and a hundred outlaws tougher than you have been trying to kill that man for years and he's still above ground. Yeah, I'm sure he's gonna kill you. I'll tell you something else that maybe you don't know or maybe you do, but just too damn stupid to understand it. There's not a soldier at Clark, there's not a homesteader around, and not too many townspeople, that don't owe Tye for helping them out. You get lucky and kill him, I guarantee one or several of them will hunt you down. Ain't that right Jason?"

Zeb turned his head slightly to the left as the man named Jason answered.

"Damn right, Jim."

Zeb hadn't noticed until now that the man named Jason and two other men had their pistols aimed at him. He reached up and tipped his hat. "See you gents around. I can't say it's been pleasant though." He turned and walked out madder than a momma bear protecting her cubs. He resented the men for 'buffaloing' him. No one had ever done that to him before. "I'll get even with those bastards when I'm thru doing what I have to do," he muttered out loud

~~.

Yahzie sat with his old friends, Too-Shay, Little Bear, and his new friend, the older and experienced Chuntz.

"The bluecoats fought better than I expected," Yahzie said. Too-Shay and Little Bear grunted their agreement.

"Yes, they fought well," Chuntz agreed, "But the difference was the scout with the repeating rifle. He's good and killed or wounded many of our friends.

"I saw him and had my sights on him twice, but I missed once and another soldier took my second bullet that was intended for him," little Bear said.

"He lives a charmed life," Yahzie said nodding his head. "He has survived for years even though he was targeted by many of our people's greatest warriors." He stood up and looked down at the three braves. "So, how do we deal with this scout, this invincible warrior?"

"Was he the one I heard about that killed Little Wolf and took the big gun?" Too-Shay asked.

Chuntz nodded. "No one saw, but who else could have done it?"

Little Bear stood up and spoke. "My father told me stories about this Watkins father. He was a great warrior and was respected among my fathers tribe-our tribe. He taught the young Watkins all that he knew just as our fathers taught us. The scout fights like an Apache, thinks like an Apache, and tracks like an Apache. He could have been a great warrior, maybe a chief if he had not been born white."

"This I have heard from my father," Yahzie said and then turned to Chuntz. "What do you think we should do? You have been in many battles with the soldiers. What would be your counsel on what we should do?"

"My council would be to make as if we are leaving and let the bluecoats think we are giving up. When they leave we can trap them another place where they are not in such a good position.

"Chuntz's counsel is good," Yahzie stated. This is what I was thinking also. The problem is that I think we lose face with the younger warriors if we did this. "

Little Bear spoke up. "This is true. They would like to attack the soldiers right now. Their mind is set on taking many scalps and more weapons."

Yahzie nodded. He turned to Chuntz. "You and I think the same my friend, but to do what I want to do, I must have these men following me. This is what we will do. We will split our men and attack from two directions at the same time. We will do this at first light. Little Bear, you and Too-Shay will take half our men and attack from the opposite hill. There is no moon tonight so have your men get as close as possible to the soldiers during the darkness.

Have your men keep their positions until I give the signal to attack. We will both attack on foot. This will make it harder on the soldiers to hit us with their bullets."

All were in agreement. Too-Shay and Little Bear left to pick their men and study the land where they would attack from while it was still light. Chuntz looked at Yahzie and put his hand on the warriors shoulder.

"We will have our victory dance tomorrow-or it will be a good day to die." He turned and left to assemble the braves that will be with him and his leader.

In a few minutes, a drum was beating a continueous180 beats per minute. **Boom** boom boom boom **Boom** boom boom boom **Boom.**

"What are they up to now?" McClellan asked his scout. "There's drums and a hell of lot of dust."

"The drums are to keep us occupied wondering when they are going to attack-keep up awake."

McClellan looked at the anxious faces of the men close top him, none who where sleeping. "It's working."

"I think the dust is from them splitting their forces. Watch down the canyon and see if you see them crossing to get behind us." Both men watched, Tye the south end and the captain the north.

~~

Back at the fort, Major Thurston was busy with the usual paperwork plus handling complaining settlers and townspeople. These problems to go along with soldiers being drunk and disorderly and a couple of desertions only made his day complete. He had dispatched Dan August, Tye's best scout and four troopers to track down and bring back the deserters. Desertion was a problem all the forts had on the frontier and probably always would have. Drills, stable duty, target practice, more drills, and dangerous patrol duty made up a soldiers life out here. The only female company was the ladies that worked the saloons and they didn't qualify for the most part as potential wives. A few did though and made a good home for the soldier.

If one added all the soldier deaths at all the forts, probably as many soldiers died from fights with other soldiers and alcoholism as from the Redman. This was not true at forts like Fort Clark which because of its location along the border had a lot more encounters than other forts in Texas.

He was short of men right now because he had dispatched thirty men, an officer and two sergeants with Corporals Lawrence and Crouch back to where McClellan was trapped about an hour ago. He would like to have sent more, but with patrols out, he was short on healthy, available soldiers. With luck and hard riding they could reach McClellan early in the morning. He prayed it wasn't too late.

Rebecca was into a regular routine now with the babies; feed every four hours and change diapers in between. She was tired, but happier than any other time in her life. She had two beautiful babies and a husband she loved more than life itself and he returned that love. She had Buff who was learning to be a grandpa at more than seventy years old and loved her and her two babies. She had Mea. O'Malley.

Mrs. O'Malley was a Godsend as far as helping her and giving her advice on certain things. And Buff, she had to smile at the sight of him changing his first soiled baby garments. The tough old mountain man almost passed out from the sight and smell, but since then he had helped, and even was doing the washing of the clothes.

She missed Tye every waking moment and prayed several times a day for his safe return. Mrs. O'Malley had just left and told her another patrol had been sent out to join McClellan's, but that's all she had said. She felt there was more to it than that, but she didn't press for more information. Maybe deep down inside, she didn't want to know if there was trouble or not. She had enough here to keep her mind occupied and besides, she knew Tye would always come back to her-he had sworn he would. She smiled as a thought crossed her mind. *"Tye is as tough a man as God ever created and not afraid of anything, but I wonder how he will handle his first job of changing dirty under garments for Nicole and Ben."* She laughed out loud.

~~

Just as Tye had predicted earlier, the weather was changing. The temperature was dropping and clouds were rolling in from the north. Buzzards were circling overhead in large numbers, waiting for the feast they were sure was coming. The dead horses lying all around the wallow where the soldiers were holed up had brought the scavengers out *"They will be a lot of dead men pretty soon too,"* Tye mused.

He looked beside him at the sleeping McClellan. He decided not to wake him just yet. *"He's had enough pain,"* he figured. He looked down the row of men and whistled softly. The men looked his way and when he got Arnolds attention, he motioned for the sergeant to come to him. Arnold was at his side quickly.

"How's the captain?"

"He won't die," Tye answered, "At least not from that wound." Arnold knew the meaning behind that last statement. "As you know," Tye continued, "it's fixing to get pretty chilly and maybe wet. You need to have some of the men get the blankets and slickers from the horses and make sure everyone has one."

"I'll take care of it right now, Tye and I'll see to it you and the captain have one."

"Thanks sergeant." Tye knew the situation they were in was going to get worse. With the cold and maybe wet weather moving in, the wounded were going to have a tough time of it. He saw a trooper coming toward him with blankets and a couple of slickers. Taking them he told the soldier to send Arnold and Garner back to him. A minute later, both men were crouched beside him.

"How's the water supply Arnold?"

"Low, Tye. The wounded have depleted it pretty badly."

"I figured as much. Here's what we need to do. Take the slickers of the dead men and spread them along the bottom of this wallow. Dig a hold in the ground under them where if it rains, the water will collect in the slickers. We can maybe get some water from them if it rains enough."

"Garner pushed the brim up on his campaign hat and smiled. "Never would have thought of that. It might just work."

"That's the reason he's the best," Arnold said over his shoulder as he left to get the slickers. "He's always thinking."

By noon, the temperature was in the fifties and a light mist began falling. Tye woke up the captain and helped him put the slicker on and then covered him with the blanket. The problem now was to keep McClellan and the other wounded from becoming chilled and catching a fever." *Just one more problem we have,"* he thought. He began to have second thought about his decision to stay here yesterday instead of making a run for it. He told himself he thought he had advised the captain correctly. The Apaches would have chosen a place more to their liking than this one. He still thought their chances were good if Lawrence and Crouch got thru to the fort. Knowing Thurston as he did, he figured the major would have another patrol on its way within an hour or so of the men's arriving. He still thought help would arrive by mid morning tomorrow He glanced at the slickers that were spread out and saw they were collecting a little water even though it was doing little more than misting right now. Looking at the clouds he knew it was going to rain pretty hard in a few minutes. Another thought occurred to him-one that brought a chill to his bones. Rain would make it hard to see and it's going to get colder later. The Apache just might try an attack while its raining.

He turned to the private next to him. "Pass the word that if it starts raining, be ready because the Apache may come with it."

Yahzie had sent a runner around the canyon to Too-Shay and Little Bear to tell them if it started to rain be ready to attack. They would now instead of in the morning. It would probably be cold and maybe even snow by then.

Twenty minutes later the rain came and with it eighty or so screaming Apaches.

Chapter Twenty Five

Your pulse is 200 plus beats per minute, your hands are shaking, and it's hard to breathe. You're sweating even though the temperature is just a little over fifty degrees and it's raining. These symptoms were what every man in the wallow felt as he waited for the Apaches they could hear screaming to break thru the wall of rain.

Tye shouted as loud as he could. "One shot with your carbine and then use your pistol." He heard the order repeated down the line, probably by Sergeant Arnold or Garner. He also had heard one the sergeants order the men to take off their slickers. That was smart because the bulky thing would hinder your movements. He knew they were in for a bad time, maybe even all would be killed. The damn rain was going to prevent them from seeing the Apaches until they were only forty or so yards away. One shot with the carbine and maybe a couple with their pistols was all he expected before they were in the wallow with them. It would then be who wanted to live the most; who was the meanest and a man can get pretty damn onery when his life is on the line.

By the sound of the screaming, the Apaches were close to breaking through the wall of rain. Tye stood up and screamed. "Men if you want to see another sunrise, you are going to have to be the toughest, meanest sonofabitches that ever lived.

The Apaches broke thru the heavy rain and were greeted by a devastating volley from both sides of the wallow. They did not slow down and were twenty- five yards from the soldiers when another volley knocked more warriors off their feet. One more deadly volley at ten yards and hell was in the wallow with the soldiers.

Tye had been firing his Henry as fast as he could work the lever and not many shots missed a target, some fatal and other only wounding. When the screaming devils came into the wallow a man could not see ten feet with the rain and smoke. Tye had his Bowie in his left hand and his Colt in his right firing at anything that moved that wasn't blue. A arm around his neck jerked him backwards and without a second hesitation, Tye stabbed backwards with the Bowie. He heard a grunt and the arm relaxed that was around his neck. He turned and shot the dying Apache in the chest. He shot another in the side of the head that was on top of McClellan.

The captain had propped himself against the wall of the wallow and shot Apaches as they came over the opposite side, at Tye's back. A trooper next to him had an arrow in his chest. McClellan picked the dead man's pistol and discarded his empty one. He shot two more Apaches as they came over the rim in front of him before a club thrown by a third warrior hit him a glancing blow on the right side of the head and everything went black.

Both sergeants were wild men and their efforts were encouraging the men around them to go crazy also. Going crazy, screaming, swinging their rifle like a club or stabbing with their knives was the only was a man was going to survive this. You had to be tougher and meaner than the Apache that was trying to kill you and that's a tall order, but to survive, that's the way it had to be.

Chuntz was determined to kill the soldier scout. He was behind the scout after bashing the skull of a trooper with his war club. Two steps away from Watkins and raising his club the scout suddenly whirled around and faced the warrior. Tye, a survivor of many a encounter with the Apache, had felt danger behind him and turned to face it. It was a gift that many fighting men had-sensing danger.

Chuntz took one more step and swung his war club arching down toward Tye's skull. Tye, instinctively, stepped toward the Apache and raising his left arm, caught Chuntz arm just below the elbow with a strong grip that surprised the warrior. Tye came up with his Bowie intended for the brave's gut but his hand was caught by the Apache's left hand. He could not wrest his hand away nor could Chuntz get his right arm loose from Tye's grip. Before the Apache could use their favorite trick of kneeing their opponent in the groin, Tye dipped a little and putting his chin on his chest sprang up catching Chuntz in the face. The Apache lost his grip and Tye droved the Bowie to the hilt in Chuntz's heart. The Apache warrior stepped back, tried to say something, but a bloody froth bubbled from his lips. He dropped to his knees and then fell face down in the dirt.

Tye picked up a Sharps rifle and with both hands on the barrel began screaming like an Apache, charged down the wallow swinging the heavy Sharps like a club. He bashed one Apache's skull in and caught another in the throat. Still screaming, he struck another warrior across the back that was on top of former Sergeant Hill. The blow was enough to stun the warrior and allowed Hill to push his knife into the man's chest. Hill stood up quickly, thankful to be alive and was going to thank Tye, but the scout was already past him, still swinging the Sharps that now had a busted stock.

It was over as suddenly as it had begun. Tye was looking for another target for his club, but saw nothing but blue clad troopers around him. He stopped, completely out of breath and sat down. Sergeant's Arnold, Garner, and several trooper came to him and patted him on the back each knowing this wild man, screaming and swinging that carbine, had turned the tide.

Arnold sat down beside his friend. "That was the damndest thing I have ever seen in my life-absolute crazy Tye. I don't think the Apache thought a white man could go as crazy as them," he chuckled and shook his head. "Crazy man, just crazy, but me and every man still alive owe their life to you my friend. Thanks."

"You're welcome," Tye said, a trace of a smile on his lips. He stood up and looked down the wallow. It was a sight that would make any man sick. Bodies were stacked on top of each other and a man could not take a step without having to step over or around one with pools of blood everywhere.

Tye turned to Sergeant Garner. "We're not out of this yet. Get a couple of men to replace those slickers and catch some water. Have the rest look after the wounded and the captain will want a casualty report and ammo count."

"Consider it done Tye." Garner conveyed the orders and men were lifting and throwing dead Apaches out of the wallow and placing their dead comrades at ne end of the wallow. The wounded were in the center being tended to by Arnold. Garner sat done and reflected on the fight. Ten minutes ago he thought it was over for him and the other soldiers. He had killed one with his Sharps and at least one with his sidearm. He had choked one to death with his bare hands, but then everywhere he looked was Apaches. Then Tye came in swinging that damn Sharps like Paul Bunyan swinging an axe and screaming his head off. He shook his head and chuckled, "I'll never doubt another story I hear about that man."

Tye sat down beside McClellan who was just regaining his senses. His shoulder was bleeding from reopening the wound he received last night and he found a couple more he didn't know he had. He had a cut on his side from what he figured was a knife, but it had already stopped bleeding and somehow, sometime in the fight he had taken a hit on the back of the head. A large bump gave proof of that.

"Ho…How…what happened?" a confused McClellan mumbled.

"Well, we are alive," Tye said. "At least some of us. It was rough captain. I have Sergeant Garner getting a casualty report."

"The Apaches?"

"I don't know how many are left. It was raining too hard to see and we were all sorter busy," he replied giving the captain a reassuring smile. "But we hurt them pretty damn bad. I don't think they will hit us again."

Garner slid in beside Tye and McClellan.

"Eighteen dead, Sir and fifteen wounded, four probably won't make it. The other wounded can still fight. We counted forty-six dead Apaches sir and I'm sure a lot more are wounded. The rain had let up considerably, but we caught enough water so far to fill several canteens thanks to Tye's idea of using the slickers. We still have plenty of ammunition both for the Sharps and the Colts."

"Thank you Sergeant Garner. Are the sounded being taken care of?"

Sergeant Arnold is a fair hand at doctoring. He's in charge of the wounded."

"Very well, Sergeant. One other thing. Make damn sure those Apaches are all dead. The ones you carried out of our little fort as well as those that were lying outside."

"Yes sir." Garner gave a quick salute and started to leave, but turned back. "Private Downey is missing sir."

"Missing! Did he desert?"

"No one is for sure. It was chaos all around and every man was busy trying to stay alive."

"Thank you sergeant."

Five minutes later the sun came out and even though it was in the fifties, the rays felt good. Steam was coming off the uniforms and Tye, looking at the sky figured the rain was over which would let the men dry out before nightfall when it would get a lot colder.

Tye stood up and found some healthy troopers. He told them to carry the dead Apaches about fifty yards out from the wallow. He knew the Apache would come back for their dead tonight and he wanted them far enough away they would not be seen by the troops. There had been enough killing this day.

The rest of the day was spent tending the wounded and making them as comfortable as possible. The dead were wrapped in blankets and a slicker wrapped around each and tied securely at both ends. It would be two more days before they reached the fort and the corpses would be getting a little ripe by then and Tye was hoping the slickers would keep the smell down some.

They would have left for the fort earlier, as soon as the fight was over if; one, it was raining even though it was only coming down half as hard as earlier and two, there were several wounded soldiers that would be a little stronger tomorrow than they were today and could handle the ride better. The third reason was the men were exhausted having not slept in over twenty-four hours plus beating off two Apache charges. Tye had the men round up several long, thick limbs for him to use in making travois for those that could not ride. He discussed the situation with the captain and was glad McClellan agreed. They could leave early in the morning after the men get some needed rest tonight.

Chapter Twenty Six

Yahzie sat on his pony and looked at what was left of his men. Many were dead and many more wounded and some of them would not see another sunset. The warriors were staying away from him, a sign they had lost faith in his medicine. His heart was heavy. Not only had he lost the fight with the soldiers, his best friend Too-Shay was dead, Little Bear was wounded badly, and Chuntz was also dead. To make matters worse, the scout Watkins was still alive and it was he that turned the Apache victory into a defeat.

He was sure the scout was protected by the Gods. He shot at him twice and missed. He saw Chuntz attack Watkins from behind and somehow Watkins knew he was there and killed him. He saw another brave swing his club at the white mans head only to hit a glancing blow when the scout turned his head for some unknown reason. *"The scout has big medicine,"* he mused. *I have no family left, no honor among my people. I have shamed my father's name.* He hung his head and wept. He wept not because he felt sorry for himself, but for the Apache and the Apache way of life. The bluecoats were good fighters and there were many more of them than Apache. The white settlers were coming like a flood, taking the land, killing what game there was.

He looked up at the sky and wondered why Ussen, the Creator, had forgotten him. He slide off his pony and walked over to his friend, Little Bear. The warrior had a hole in his stomach where a soldier bullet had entered. Yahzie had seen many wounds like this and knew his friend would shortly be in the other world. He knelt beside his friend and put his hand on the brave's forehead. He almost jerked it away because it was so hot.

Little Bear's eyes fluttered, and then opened.

"It is good you are alive my friend," he said, his voice barely above a whisper. He barely had the strength to lift his hand and place it on Yahzie's arm. "We rode many trails and shared many campfires my brother," he said. There was a pause and he shut his eyes trying to get the strength to continue. It was painful for Yahzie to watch his friend suffer. Little Bear continued. "Did Too-Shay…" Yahzie shook his head. Little Bear, learning his friend was dead, shut his eyes. He spoke with his eyes closed and Yahzie had to put his ear close to his friend's lips to hear his words.

Struggling for each word he said, "You have been a good and loyal friend my brother. You must continue the fight against the…" his hand slipped from Yahzie's arm. He took a deep breath, exhaled slowly-and died.

Yahzie dropped his chin on his chest as a single tear rolled down his cheek. He kneeled there for several minutes, grieving, until he heard horses. Looking up he saw his braves approaching him. Stopping a few feet from him, one told him they would stay and gather their dead after dark and then they were leaving this place that would forever be known as The Canyon of the Dead to all Apaches.

About midnight the Apache warriors made their way on silent feet to where their brothers had been placed by the soldiers. They quickly picked them up and made their way away from this place of death. They would bury their friends in the mountains of Mexico, their homeland, the place sacred to the Apache.

Yahzie stayed. He had decided what he must do. It would be done at dawn.

The soldiers were getting some much needed rest. Sentries were posted and changed every two hours. Tye would take the last watch, the one before sunrise. He slept soundly, exhausted from the last twenty-fou r hours. He slept sitting up with his back against the wall of the wallow.

Dawn found Tye and Sergeant Arnold on the last watch. One of the wounded troopers had died during the night, but the other wounded had gained a little strength and would probably make the trip back to Clark. It appeared it was going to be a beautiful sunrise, one that most of the men yesterday didn't think they would live to see.

The sun was breaking over the eastern hills when Tye saw him-a lone Apache sitting on a horse. Out of the corner of his eye he saw a soldier raising his carbine. "Hold your fire soldier. Put the sharps down," he said sternly. Then he spoke louder, "No one shoot at that Indian."

Tye stood up and climbed out of the wallow.

"What are you doing?" McClellan asked.

"I'm betting that Apache is the leader of that bunch, Yahzie. I'm going to see what he wants, captain."

"What if there is other Apaches waiting for someone dumb enough to go up there." McClellan immediately wished he had not said it that way.

Tye looked back at the captain, smiled said, "Thanks for the compliment. I'll be back in a few minutes-unless there are other Apaches up there, then we may have a problem." McClellan started to say something, but Tye had already turned away and started up the slope where the Apache sat on his pony.

As Tye walked up the slope toward the Apache his eyes were searching every bush, rock, and any other place that could hide an Apache. He saw the Apache slide off the paint and start walking toward him. They stopped ten yards apart. He saw the warrior had no weapon in his hand, but had a knife in a beaded sheath on his hip.

"Waa-kins? The Apache questioned.

Tye nodded. He pointed to the warrior and said "Yahzie?"

Yahzie nodded, pleased that the great scout knew his name. "Talk," he said in Spanish.

Tye knew some Spanish and he asked Yahzie to sit and tell him what he wanted. He listened as Yahzie told the story in Spanish and in sign language of the six men who came into his camp and killed his family while he was away hunting. He told of tracking the men killing three of them and wounding the others. Tye said he had spoke to two of the men and told him the story of what they said about the Apache killing their friend at the junction of the Pecos and Rio Grande River.

Tye was not surprised when the Apache told him that one of the men shot their friend and killed him. He did take the dead man's horse though. Tye told him the men were being held until he returned to Fort Clark.

"What will they do to them," Yahzie asked.

Tye knew nothing would be done because no white man was going to be charged for killing an Apache. He thought for a moment before answering.

"If you could get your hands on these men would you go back to Mexico and never return to Texas?"

"Yahzie stood up. "The days of the Apache are numbered Watkins. This, I think you know."

Tye nodded. "It is sad that this is true. I respect the Apache way of life. It is a good life, but the white man is like the stars, too many to count. They want this land to raise their families. I know your people have roamed this land and called it your own for many years. If I was Apache, I would be like you, fighting to keep what is mine.

Times are changing and if your people do not change-they will be no more Apache left. This I would hate to see."

Yahzie believed what the scout said came from his heart. "I have heard this about you, that you are a white man who understands the Apache. My heart is glad to find this about you is true. My own heart is heavy with the plight of my people. We do not know what to do, what direction to go- so we fight. You say my people must change. What does this mean?"

Tye paused for a few seconds, carefully mulling over what he was going to say, but he could think of no other way to say what must be said except straight forward and to the point. "The Apache must give up the warpath and adapt to the ways of the white man." He saw Yahzie stiffen at his words, but the warrior said nothing. "The Apache way of life is coming to an end. In both our hearts, we know this to be true. Your people must take up the ways of the white man and grow crops to eat or raise cattle and horses. They must build homes in which they can raise their families instead of moving all the time." He paused for a minute to let his words sink in before continuing. "When I was young there was no problem between the white man and the Apache. My best friend was an Apache boy my age by the name of Nasay. It could be that way again."

Yahzie stood even straighter, a flash of anger, or was it pride, showing. "Why is it the Apache must change everything and the white man nothing?"

"That is the way it is Yahzie. The one who is victorious sets the rules. I know the white man has not won yet, but as we both agreed earlier, it is only a matter of time. The longer that time is the more men, women, and children will die-both white and Apache."

Yahzie knew this was true. The Apache were few compared to the white man. He slumped a little, some of the promptness leaving him. He sat down motioning for Tye to sit with him. "I can take your words to council with the elders. They are wise and know in their hearts your words are true, but I don't think the young ones will listen. They want to live as their father's did. They would say the white man will not keep their word and let the Apache live in peace."

"This is true. There are white men who would not forget the past, but there are Apache who would not forget also."

Yahzie nodded. "There are many among my people who will fight to the end-those too blind, or too proud, to face the truth. I was one of those until this day. Until this morning I wanted nothing more than to kill you, the great army scout, the Apache killer, and make your family and those of the bluecoat's families feel how I felt when I lost my family. Let them grieve the way I did. I wanted to kill the men who killed my family. I felt that is the only way I could find peace in my heart. Killing the three men and other white men and women as well as many soldiers has not done so." He looked past Tye, staring off in the distance, but not seeing anything. "I'm tired of fighting, of watching my friends die. I am ready to seek peace." Tye sat, saying nothing. He figured the best thing to do was to let the man get everything off his chest

"You say you could arrange for me to meet the two men being held."

Tye nodded. He didn't not know how he would do it, but he would somehow. "You have my word."

" If I could see the two men that remain alive that took my family from me punishcd, I would never come to Texas again. This is my word."

"I have seen what I heard is true about Yahzie being a great warrior and I believe Yahzie's word is good. Yahzie has my word that if you follow us unseen by the others back to Fort Clark, I will see to it that the two men leave the fort. What happens to them-or you I will have nothing to do with after they leave. This is my word to you."

Yahzie, hearing the scout's praising his fighting ability, stood straight as an arrow, arms folded across his chest and his chin jutting out. "Watkins word is good. I will watch for them on the road north from Clark." He turned to leave, but turned back to the scout. "Maybe if more white men were like you, there would be no trouble between our people." He walked back to the pony and in one fluid motion, was atop of the horse and rode away without looking back.

Tye let out a breath of relief. *"When I saw him sitting there alone., I figured he was going to charge us and die like an Apache warrior or he was going to call me out and challenge me to a fight to the death. After seeing him up close, it would have been one hell of a fight."*

Chapter Twenty Seven

The relief patrol arrived two hours after daylight with extra horses and medical supplies. The wounded were treated and the dead, wrapped in the rain slickers, were tied across the backs of horses. They were ready to leave within an hour but McClellan said they would wait another two hours so the horses could recuperate a little after the hard march from Clark.

There were many stories of the fight from the men of McClellan's patrol passed around to their friends of the relief patrol. The one repeated the most was Tye's screaming, crazed-like Apache charge down the wallow swinging the Sharps carbine like a club and whopping Apaches left and right. To a man, each said that one act inspired them to fight harder when each thought all was lost.

Tye sat with the injured McClellan who was in a lot of pain from the knife wound, discussing the fight and Tye's talk with Yahzie.

After the discussion McClellan asked a question. "What makes you think Yahzie will keep his word and not come back into Texas?

"He is an Apache, captain. In all my years of knowing them, fighting them, I have never had one lie to me. When you boil everything down and get past their reputation as being brutal, they are an honorable people. They are brought up respecting their elders and being honest in every way. I know you know that cannot be said for the white man. The one thing an Apache cannot stand, besides cowardice, is a man who lies. Old Buff, who has had experiences with a lot of different tribes, says that is true of all Indians. They all love their families, respect their elders, and honest in all things."

"Well, I hope you are right because I don't want to face a bunch led by him again. Do you think the major will go along with your plan to let the two men go?"

Tye nodded. "I think so. He cannot hold them for killing Apaches and he probably can't find out where the money came from they had in their saddlebags. I'm sure he will be glad to rid himself of the two and let fate take care of them."

McClellan, as painful as his shoulder was, made sure everything was ready to leave. With Tye's help, he managed to get mounted in the saddle and they moved out, heading for Clark.

~~

Zeb Cates was doing what he had been doing for the last two days-sitting in a saloon, drinking and when he could find a game, playing poker. He had never been confused before in his life. He always knew what he wanted and how he was going to get it. Now, one minute he wanted to kill Watkins and the next he wasn't so sure. Every damn cowboy, soldier, trapper, and every other man in this hell hole of a town thought the man hung the moon. Word was out that he wouldn't live long enough to meet the scout again, but so far it had only been men talking that had one too many drinks like the trapper he had taken some money off of earlier. The man had been drunk and accused Zeb of cheating and went for his gun. Zeb could have killed him and everyone would have to say it was a fair fight, but the drunk was slow so Zeb caught him flush on the chin with a hard right fist and the argument was over. Later, when the man regained his senses, he said he would get Zeb.

He leaned back in his chair, his back against the saloon wall. Now the major was another story. He would do what he said he would do if I killed Watkins and I'm sure it would harder than hell for me to get out of Texas in one piece. He slammed his glass down, spilling what little rot-gut was left in it. Pouring himself another, he thought about his nephews, Yancey and Billy.

"Now there's a pair for you; killers and rapist through and through and here I am, probably going to get my ass killed trying to avenge them. He stood up quickly, but had to grab the table for a second to steady himself. He had made his decision. *"I'll be dammed if I am going to die for them two. I'm headed back home tomorrow."* He walked out the door, sniffed the evening air, and felt better for having made up his mind. He walked to the Sargent Hotel and ordered supper.

~~

Two of the wounded took a turn for the worse so McClellan ordered a forced march back to Clark, stopping only occasionally to rest the horses. They rode into Brackett at midmorning. The first thing Tye saw was four men grouped around a man. From what was being said it was apparent it was not a friendly meeting.

Tye rode over and was surprised when he saw the man in the middle was Cates. He sat there for a moment trying to get a grasp of what was happening. The others were men he hadn't saw before but knew from their clothes they were trappers and probably hard cases. He dismounted and walked toward the men. *"This is a hell of a situation,"* he mused. *"I figure me and Cates are headed for a showdown and here I am considering helping the man out."*

Zeb saw the scout coming toward him and wondered what he was doing. *"I guess he will join in the fun and make damn sure I get the hell beat out of me,"* he thought.

Tye pushed one of the trappers aside and stepped in the ring of men with Cates.

"Got a little trouble Cates?"

"Looks like I got a handful. This one here," he said pointing to the man he had knocked out the day before, "is one sorry-ass poker player and brought his friends here to collect his losings."

"Never thought much of a man who has to get his friends to help him in a fight and sure never liked four against one. You ready Mr. Cates?" Tye asked   still wondering what in the dickens he was doing helping this man who was threatening to kill him the last time he saw him.

"I sure as hell am," Zeb said relieved that the big man wasn't there to beat the hell out of him again. He uncorked a right that caught one of the men on the chin knocking him on his back.

Two of the men jumped Tye-their mistake. He hit the one in front a terrific blow just above the belt doubling the man over. The second man came from behind and had his arm around Tye's neck. Tye turned his body slightly and rammed his elbow in the man's belly. The grip on Tye's neck loosened slightly so with his left hand, Tye grabbed a handful of the man's long hair and at the same time, dipped his shoulder and threw the man over his shoulder. Everyone watching heard the wind go out of the trapper as he hit the ground hard on his back. The first man was back in the fight and pulled his knife. Tye kicked out hard with his right foot slamming it into the man's left knee. With a scream, the man hit the ground holding his busted knee. Tye turned to help Zeb, but he didn't have to.

Zeb had hit the fourth man in the stomach and as he doubled over, caught the man flush in the face with his knee. Two of the men were out cold, one was still trying to catch his breath, and the other man was lying on the ground, moaning and holding his broke knee. It was over in less than ten seconds.

"Let me buy you a beer," Zeb said, shaking Tye's hand.

"Let me go see my wife and babies first. I'll see you in about an hour at Jims."

"After things I have said, Jim won't let me in his place."

"Just sit on the porch then. We'll go in when I get there." He mounted Sandy and crossed the bridge over Los Moras Creek with the men. After reporting to Thurston, he headed home to see Rebecca, the kids, and old Buff. After explaining everything to the major, he was glad that the commander had agreed with his plan.

In fact he was elated with Tye's plan. The men deserved to be punished, but he had no reason to hold them.

"Maybe the Apache will give them what they deserve," he said to Tyc.

"I don't think there's a doubt about that, sir," Tye replied smiling. "If that's all sir, I think I'll go see my wife and kids before I escort those two out of town.

"After a few minutes with Rebecca and the kids and promising to be back shortly, Tye and Buff went to the guard house to get the two men. They took them to the stables and after they saddled their horses, took them to the road leading north out of Brackett. Tye took the bullets out of their guns before handing them to the two men and sent them on their way telling them not to come back. Tye watched them for a moment as they rode off loading their guns and Henry's.

"I would like to see what happens," He mused, *"but I promised the little lady I would be back in an hour or so.* He and Buff headed to Jims where they saw Cates sitting on the porch whittling something with his knife. Cates looked up as the two men approached him. Standing up, he threw the piece of wood down and stuck the knife back in its sheath.

"Ready to buy me that beer?" Tye asked.

"If the owner will let me in with you," Cates answered as they walked thru the bat-wing doors of Jim's place. Jim had a startled look on his face, but said nothing as the three men sat down at a table.

"Zeb," Tye said, "this here old codger is Shakespeare McDovitt."

"Most people call me Buff," Buff said shaking the man's hand.

"Glad to meet you," Zeb said taking Buff's hand. "Someone told me about you . Said you were a genuine mountain man."

"I trapped my share of Beaver back then."

"Buff was my pa's best friend back in the Rockies, Zeb. They trapped together for about eight or nine years. Buff came here to see me about a year or so ago and Rebecca and me wouldn't let him leave."

Jim sat the beers down and gave a questioning look at Tye, but the scout just smiled at him so the owner of the saloon went back behind the bar and minded his own business.

"Always wondered about those days. Must've been nice to be as carefree as one could be-at least that's what the novels said."

"It was a good life if a man didn't freeze to death, starve to death, get eaten by a grizz, or get his hair lifted by the Blackfoot," Buff chuckled.

"My father's brother left home in twenty-five. He wanted to be a mountain man. My father never heard from him again."

Buff scratched the back of neck while he pondered the name of Cates. "Your pa's brother wasn't Gabriel Cates was it?

Zeb straightened up. "You knew him?"

"Not really. I met him once. Heard tell he was a mighty fine man to trap with. Hear he got himself kilt by some Blackfeet. I think that was about '32 or '33.

Zeb leaned back in his chair and smiled. "I guess he did make it after all. My pa should would like to have known that." He looked at Tye and chuckled. "See. Not all of us Cates are bad-asses like Yancey and Billy."

"And Zeb," Tye said laughing.

Zeb laughed too. "I guess I deserved that." He leaned forward and rested his elbows on the table. "I ran my mouth a lot when I got here Tye. Said a lot of things about what I was going to do an all. That was before I started hearing all the stories about those two nephews of mine and the stories about you. I found out the hard way that the stories were true about you." He rubbed his chin. "I'd say you beat some sense in me," he added laughing. "I was headed to get my horse and leave this country when that old trapper showed up with his friends. I was gonna eat crow and go home."

"What are you going to do back home?" Tye asked.

Zeb shrugged his shoulders. "Don't know for sure. The old home place is gone, my family scattered who know where."

"You were an officer in the war?"

"How did you know that?"

"Just a hunch. Some of your mannerisms told me you probably were.?

Zeb nodded. I had the rank of captain. Saw a lot my men get killed."

"Have you given any thought to joining the army? You could be a sergeant real quick I bet."

Zeb let out a howl that could be heard down the street at the next saloon. Everyone in Jim's turned their heads to see what was so funny. "Me-a Yankee soldier and wear that blue uniform?"

"Why not?"

Zeb looked at Tye. "You're serious ain't you.?"

"Army needs good men and certainly men with your experience," Tye said. "The Indian trouble is far from over and the bandit gangs out here are as bad as the Apache. The army needs older, experienced men that have seen about everything there is too see to hold the young ones in line when things get tough. You fit that bill pretty well I'd say."

Zeb leaned back and picked at the sleeve of his shirt. "Blue, huh. Maybe I could live with that. What's the pay?"

"Thirteen dollars a month, three meals a day, except when on patrol, and all the bullets you need plus a horse and tack. There's the extra thing also, a great chance to see the country side and lots of fresh air."

"And get killed by some damn bandit or scalped by an Apache?" Zeb said laughing.

"You have to take the good with the bad Zeb."

Cates sat there thinking, his fingers rapping the table to some tune, probably a Rebel tune Tye mused.

"Let's do it," Cates said finally. "I'll sign up."

"Let's go see the major," Tye said.

After Cates was sworn in Tye and Buff headed home. It had been quite a week. The problem of the Apache had been ended, at least temporarily, the problem of what to do with the two men had been solved-at least he figured it had if Yahzie had followed them to the fort. Tye was ready to spend some time with Rebecca and for the first time in his life, spend some time being a father.

Epilogue

Three days had passed since the battered patrol came back from the fight with Yahzie and his band of Apaches. Tye had spent ever waking moment with Rebecca and the babies and he loved being a doting father.

Today, after a mid-day meal and Ben and Nicole were asleep, he told Rebecca he needed to check on a matter and would be back well before dark. She didn't ask what the *matter* was, but she suspected the reason. Tye had told her about the agreement with Yahzie and she knew that sooner or later he would need to know what happened. He asked Buff is he wanted to go and the old trapper was more than happy to go. It had been awhile since he had sat in the saddle and he was sure his old bones would remind him of his age tomorrow.

About four miles from Brackett and just into the low hills, Tye spotted four buzzards circling a quarter mile west of the road. A few minutes later he and Buff were looking at the two men they had escorted out of town.

The two men were spread eagle on the ground, their hands and feet were tied to stakes driven into the ground. Dismounting, the two men both felt sick to their stomach at the sight before them. Both men had been scalped while they were still alive. Ants were crawling in and out of their mouths, nose and in the sockets where their eyes had been.

"I'd say that was one upset Apache," Buff said.

"I'd say he had a damn good reason," Tye answered. "I could do worse than that to anyone who hurt Rebecca or the kids, or you." Buff looked at his friend and saw by his expression he was serious.

"Let's head back," Tye said mounting Sandy.

"You gonna leave them like that?"

"Hell yes!" Tye said emphatically. "Feeding the buzzards and ants is probably the only good thing those two ever done." He looked at Buff who was trying to get his foot in the stirrup. "Need some help getting in the saddle old timer," he said laughing.

Buff got his left foot in the stirrup and swung his right over the saddle settling his rear in the hard leather. "When we get back, I might just show you how old I am when I tan your butt for your smart mouth." Both men had a good laugh and headed back home to Rebecca and the kids.

Book Nine of the Tye Watkins Series

Tye, after fighting Apaches for the last fifteen years, has decided to change professions. He had a family now and decided his current job as a scout was just too dangerous. He had an offer a year ago from the Governor of Texas to become a United States Marshall so he had Rebecca write a letter inquiring if the offer was still on the table.

It had been and Tye had just returned from receiving his appointment as a United States Deputy Marshall. He knew chasing outlaws and serving warrants would be dangerous, but no way as hazardous as tracking Apaches. He would learn that some white men were more dangerous and treacherous than any Apache.

His first assignment was finding a man named Jack Gillespie better known as Bloody Jack. He was a robber and murderer and would lead Tye on a long and dangerous chase.

Gary McMillan